SINK OR SWIM

SARAH MLYNOWSKI

ORCHARD

ORCHARD BOOKS
Carmelite House
50 Victoria Embankment
London EC4Y 0DZ

First published in 2013 in the United States by Scholastic Press,
an imprint of Scholastic Inc., Publishers since 1920. scholastic,
scholastic press, and associated logos are trademarks and/or
registered trademarks of Scholastic Inc.

This edition published by Orchard Books in 2015

ISBN 978 1 40833 420 1

A CIP catalogue record for this book is available
from the British Library.

1 3 5 7 9 8 6 4 2

Printed in Great Britain by CPI Group (UK) Ltd, Croydon, CR0 4YY

Orchard Books is an imprint of Hachette Children's Group,
and published by The Watts Publishing Group Limited,
an Hachette UK company.

www.hachette.co.uk

For Anabelle,

my littlest princess

✳ *Chapter One* ✳

My Parents Are in the Way

S hould I pack a swimming costume?
Yes. I definitely should.

I stuff my swimming costume – it's pale blue with sweet white ruffles – into my bright-red suitcase. I'm going to visit my nana in Chicago! I can't wait. My nana is the best. Chicago is the best. And, yeah, I know it's cold to be swimming in Chicago, but my nana lives in a block of flats with an indoor pool and a hot tub.

I'm not really into pools, since I'm not the world's best swimmer.

But hot tubs? I love hot tubs. What's not to love about a big, bubbling bath that melts all your worries away?

Mum and I are flying to Chicago this Friday, only three days from today. It's a long weekend, so I won't miss any school, which is important because I am not a fan of missing school. I am an excellent note-taker and I like hearing everything the teachers say. Also, I don't want to give my new friends the opportunity to forget about me.

So far I have packed:

- the swimming costume
- two bottoms (one pair of jeans, one pair of stretchy black leggings)
- three pairs of undies
- three tops (one purple hooded jumper, one white jumper, one light-green T-shirt with a collar)
- two pairs of pyjamas (my orange pair and my navy pair – not my favourites, but they're practically all I have left; I am dangerously low on pyjamas.)

The reason I am low on pyjamas: when the magic mirror in our basement took my seven-year-old brother, Jonah, and me to Zamel (where we met Snow White), I accidentally left behind my lime-green pjs. When the magic mirror in our basement then took us to Floom (where we met Cinderella), I accidentally left behind my polka-dot pink-and-purple ones.

Yes, we have a magic mirror in our basement. It came with the house.

I open my jewellery box. My nana bought me a pretty mother-of-pearl necklace for my tenth birthday and I think I should pack it. I don't really understand what the difference between pearl and mother-of-pearl is, to be honest. My nana said mother-of-pearl was more age-appropriate for me. Personally, I think they should call it *child-of-pearl* if they want it to be more age-appropriate. Anyway, I don't normally wear the necklace to school because I'm afraid it will catch on something and all the mother-of-pearls will go flying across the classroom. But it'll be safe in my suitcase.

My nana bought me my jewellery box, too. The outside features images of all the fairy tale characters. Like Rapunzel with her long hair, the Little Mermaid with her tail, Cinderella in her poofy baker's hat, and Snow White in my lime-green pyjamas. Cinderella and Snow White weren't always dressed like that, obviously. Only after Jonah and I changed the endings of their stories. Which was a total accident. We didn't *mean* to change the fairy tales. But everything ended up okay, so no need to worry.

I gently place the mother-of-pearl necklace on top of my navy pjs. I really need to go shopping. But what am I going to tell my parents about my missing pyjamas? Maybe that the dryer ate them? It's not like I can tell them *the truth*; Gabrielle, the fairy who lives inside the magic mirror in Snow White's world, told us not to. Maryrose, the fairy who lives inside our mirror, has never said a word to us – so who knows what she thinks?

Last Thursday, Jonah and I woke up just before midnight with the full intention of either talking to Maryrose or getting her to take us to another fairy tale.

We got dressed. We sneaked down the stairs. We opened the basement door.

And we saw that the lights were on.

My parents were in the basement.

My parents were not supposed to be in the basement at midnight.

Sure, *technically* the basement is their home office. So of course they are *allowed* to work in it. But how were we supposed to get sucked into the magic mirror when our parents were awake and standing right there? We couldn't. It was a problem.

Why were my parents working at the ridiculous hour of midnight? No, they do not work for a twenty-four-hour call centre. They do not work for a bakery, either, and they are not getting up to make the doughnuts. Or brownies. (Or crownies. That's an inside joke between us and Cinderella.)

No, my parents started their own law firm when we moved to Smithville a few months ago. And now they're working like crazy people. Jonah and I haven't been able to get to the mirror all week. My parents had a lot more free time when we lived in Chicago.

Now I sit down at my desk and take out my maths textbook and notebook. Time for homework. This desk was with me in my old bedroom back in Chicago, but it looks different – bigger – in my new room. I'm still kind of getting used to my new house. I'm not going to lie – it helps that I have a magic mirror.

It also helps that I've made new friends here: Robin and Frankie. Frankie is a girl, although I know it doesn't sound like it. When I have a little girl, I am not going to give her a boy's name. It's too confusing. On the first day of school, Ms Hellman, the PE teacher, divided up our class into boys and girls and put Frankie with the boys. Frankie's face turned the colour of a tomato.

We laugh about it now, though. The three of us: Frankie, Robin and me, Abby. We're a trio. The terrific trio. Or maybe the tremendous trio. Or… I can't think of another word that means awesome that starts with T. There would be a lot more options if we were four or five. Fantastic four. Fabulous four. Famous four. Fun four. But two new friends are good. Two friends are great.

You get what you get and you don't get upset, right? That's what my mother always says. That and: There's nothing to fear but fear itself. And also: You've made your bed, now you have to sleep in it.

For the record, I make my bed every morning. Unlike my brother.

Anyway, I'm going to use all those expressions when I'm a judge. Oh, yeah, I'm going to be a judge when I grow up. Well, first I'm going to be a lawyer, and then I'm going to be a judge, because that's the rule.

I pretend my pencil is a gavel and bang it against my maths textbook. 'That's my ruling and it's final!' I say out loud. Not bad.

My door swings open and Jonah barges into my room. 'What are you doing?'

'Homework,' I say.

'Then why are you talking to yourself?'

'Because I feel like it,' I snap, embarrassed that he caught me.

He sits on my bed and swings his legs. 'Why is your stuff already in your suitcase?'

I turn around to face him. 'Why would it not be? Why are you asking me a million questions?'

'I'm bored,' he says. 'Want to see if we can rock-climb up the side of the house?'

'No, Jonah, I do not. I have to finish my homework, and then I want to finish packing. I'm leaving in three days, you know.'

My dad's friend from college and his son are coming to visit this weekend, so my mum and I thought it was the perfect time for some girl bonding. But even if my brother was coming to Chicago, he is the kind of person who would pack the morning of a big trip, not three days before. Actually I take that back. My brother would not pack *at all* because my parents would not trust him to pack. Last time we went away for a weekend, he packed one pair of underpants, two socks, and Kadima paddles. No T-shirts. No jeans. No shoes.

'I don't think you have to pack,' Jonah says. 'I heard Mum telling Dad that she's exhausted and that her brain is getting fuzzy and that she should probably postpone the trip to Chicago until after the case.'

I jump out of my chair. 'What? Postpone the trip? *Noooo!*'

He shrugs his thin little shoulders. 'Sorry, that's what I heard.'

'Are they in the basement?'

Jonah nods.

I run right out of the room and down the two flights of stairs.

13

Jonah is on my tail. We reach the basement in approximately two seconds flat.

'Mum!' I shout.

I can't help but glance at the mirror. It's still attached to the wall with heavy Frankenstein bolts. Same stone frame engraved with small fairies with wings and wands. Nothing has changed.

Good.

'Yes, honey?' my mum asks, swivelling her chair to face me.

I turn away from the mirror fast before my parents see me staring and realise it's a magic mirror that slurps us up into fairy tales.

No, they probably wouldn't guess all that just by seeing me look at it. Especially since they're so preoccupied with work that they haven't noticed that I'm short two pairs of pyjamas, or that their law books are gone from the basement bookcases, or that we're missing one swivel chair. Actually, the swivel chair they noticed, but they just assumed they'd left it in Chicago. The truth is all these things got sucked into the mirror when we visited Snow White.

Anyway. 'Mum. Please don't tell me we're cancelling the trip to Chicago. Please, please, please don't.'

'Oh, honey,' my mum says, her forehead wrinkling.

14

'I'm sorry. I was going to talk to you about it tonight, but...'

'No buts!' I cry. 'It's too late to change your mind. Nana is expecting us! We already have plane tickets! And I already packed!' I stomp my foot on the floor for effect. I know it's babyish, but I can't help myself.

'I spoke to Nana this morning – she understands. She said we should come the next long weekend. And I called the airline and we can switch our tickets, too. Maybe then Dad and Jonah can come with us. We'll stay in a hotel and everything!'

Tears fill my eyes. 'I don't want to wait until next time! Next time is months away. And I don't want to stay in a hotel. I want to stay with Nana.'

She shakes her head. 'I'm sorry, honey. But I'm just too busy. Please try to understand.'

I don't want to understand. I cross my arms. I pout. I stomp my foot one more time, just because I feel like it.

I don't want to act like a baby, but...but...but... Sigh. I know my mum is really busy. And it's my job as the older sibling to act mature. I am ten, after all.

'I *am* sorry,' my mum says. 'But you know what they say. You get what you get, and you don't—'

'Get upset,' I grumble.

Although right now, it's a saying I wish I could *forget*.

15

✳ *Chapter Two* ✳

Grumpy Pants

T hat night, I toss and turn and turn and toss. I can't
sleep.

My still-packed suitcase is sitting on my floor. Seeing it
there just makes everything worse, but I don't have the
heart to unpack it.

It's 11:45 P.M. and my dad and mum are asleep. They
turned in about an hour ago.

Hmm.

I feel a tingle in my belly.

I may not be able to visit my nana, but I can definitely visit fairy land.

I sit up and push my covers off. Yes! I'm going to visit fairy land right now. Why not? I'm wide awake. My parents are not in the basement. Tonight is the night. I know it. I should go!

I look down at the pair of pyjamas I'm wearing. Maybe I should change into normal clothes. Although last time, the mirror finally let us in *because* of the pyjamas I was wearing. They were the same design as the Floom flag: pink with purple polka dots. But how do I know what clothes will help us get into the mirror if I don't know what story we're going to?

I guess I'll stay in my pyjamas. That way if the mirror doesn't let us in, I can at least go straight back to bed.

I spot my open suitcase. Oh! I'll bring my suitcase with me! Why?

1. We are usually in the stories at least a few days. I may as well have a change of clothes with me.
2. It's already packed.
3. Maybe something inside will help us get into the mirror.

So the suitcase is coming, too. I strap on my watch

17

(last time I forgot it and had no idea how much time had passed), then zip my bag and wheel it into Jonah's room.

He's fast asleep.

'Hey!' I say, gently shaking him. 'Mum and Dad are sleeping. Let's go and see the mirror.'

He opens his left eye then sits up. 'Sure! But why are you bringing your suitcase?'

'To have extra clothes. You can put some of your stuff in it, too.'

He climbs out of bed and disappears into his cupboard. 'Like Kadima paddles?' he asks.

My brother is obsessed with playing Kadima. I do not know why. When I'm on the beach, I like to read and relax, not chase a bouncy blue ball with wooden paddles.

'I was thinking more along the lines of clean underwear, jeans and a T-shirt. You know what, I'll pack for you. You put on your trainers.'

(My trainers are already on and the laces are double-knotted.)

I pack two pairs of his Batman underpants, one pair of jeans, one blue T-shirt, our toothbrushes and cinnamon toothpaste. Then I tiptoe down the stairs to the main floor. I lift my suitcase up so that it doesn't bump and wake my parents. It is SO heavy. I motion for Jonah to grab the other end, but he's too focused on his tiptoeing to notice.

18

I stop at the landing and take a deep breath – there's no sound from our parents' bedroom. We've come so far – we can't get caught now. I open the basement door, turn on the lights, and then we creep down the rest of the way.

In front of us is the antique mirror, twice the size of me. The glass is clear and smooth. My brother and I are in the reflection, of course. We're both wearing pyjamas and trainers. What's worse – we're wearing matching black-and-white pyjamas. I hadn't noticed in Jonah's dark bedroom. We look like twins. Like Oompa Loompas. Like Dr Seuss's Thing One and Thing Two.

'We look like zebras!' Jonah says. His short brown hair is a mess. It's standing up in different directions. I pat down my own curly brown hair. I like to look neat. Also, not identical to Jonah.

I try to look deeper into the mirror to see if I can see Maryrose. She lives inside. At least, we think she lives inside. We don't really know that much about her. Only that she's a fairy and that when we knock three times, she takes us inside different fairy tales. Sometimes. I hope we're wearing – or have with us – the right thing.

'I'll do the knocking,' Jonah says. 'Ready?'

This had better work. It will be pretty annoying if I have to drag this suitcase all the way back upstairs tonight.

'One—'

'Wait! Jonah?'

His hand freezes in midair. 'Yeah?'

'Let's try not to mess up the story again, 'kay? We just want to visit and see what's happening. We don't want to change anything.'

'Uh-huh,' he says. 'One—'

'Don't "uh-huh" me,' I say. 'I do not want you touching ANYTHING or talking to ANYONE. Not without my permission. Got it?'

'Yes, Mum.'

I wag my finger. 'No messing the story up. That's a rule.'

He twists his bottom lip. 'What story do you think it'll be?'

'Hmm. I don't know.'

'I like *Jack and the Beanstalk*.' His eyes widen. 'How cool would it be to meet a giant?'

I nod. As long as he doesn't step on us.

'Or Aladdin! Then we could fly on a magic carpet.'

Flying on a magic carpet sounds a little scary. What if I fall off? On the other hand, then I wouldn't need airplanes. 'I could take the magic carpet to visit Nana!'

Jonah grunts. 'So I can't talk to anyone or touch anything, but you can steal the magic carpet and take it to Chicago?'

20

'I was kidding,' I say. Kind of.

He shifts from foot to foot. 'Can we go now?'

'Yes. Just remember: no touching.'

'Unless it's stealing a magic carpet.'

'Right.' Then I shake my head. 'No. No touching. No stealing. No anything.'

He laughs. 'Okay, okay. Can I do my three knocks now?'

'Go.'

He does. Almost immediately, there's a hissing sound. The mirror starts swirling and casts a purple light over the room. A second later, it's pulling us towards it like it's a hoover.

'It's working!' Jonah exclaims.

'Then let's go!' I grip Jonah's arm with one hand, my suitcase with the other, and step inside.

✴ *Chapter Three* ✴

Splash

The second I go through the mirror, I inhale a mouthful of water.

What is happening? Am I in the bath? Why can't I breathe?

Everything is blurry, and my eyes sting, so I close them. The water is salty. Bath water isn't salty. Also, I'm horizontal, on my stomach, and my elbows are rubbing against the ground.

A sandy ground.

Need air! Can't breathe! Lungs exploding!

I open my eyes, look for the light, and push my face towards it.

And then...*cough, cough, cough!* Ahhhhhhhh.

Air. I'm breathing air. Gulps and gulps of air. Who knew air could taste so good? Who needs ice cream when air is so incredibly delicious?

Once I've finished gorging on the air – it's an all-I-can-eat air buffet! – I realise I'm looking at a sandy beach. But I'm not on the beach. I'm in the water, looking at the beach. It's bright out here, too – around noon. What is going on? I twist around and see that a huge wave is about to smash into me. 'No!' I yell, and try, unsuccessfully, to get out of its way.

CRASH.

No, no, no, I will not drown! *Cough, cough, cough!*

My heart is thumping, and I push myself to my feet before I can get attacked again. What in the world is happening?

I turn back to face the beach. It's empty. No tourists, no sand castles, no bright-coloured beach towels. Just pure-white sand sparkling in the midday sun. Beyond the beach are trees and beyond the trees are mountains. When I turn the other way, there's blue ocean as far as the eye can see. Even as far as my *stinging* eyes can see. Wait a sec. One thing my eyes can't see is my brother.

'Jonah! Jonah, where are you?' Where is he? My heart sinks to the ocean floor.

Just as I'm about to really panic, he bursts out of the water and gives me a thumbs-up. 'How cool is this?' he cries, sopping wet and grinning.

He's here! He's okay! Hurray! 'Jonah, get over here now!'

'I'm fine!' he yells back.

Unlike me, my brother loves to swim.

According to my parents, when I was a kid, not only did I refuse to swim in the ocean, but I would cry hysterically when anyone else tried to. My parents. My brother. Strangers. Obviously I'm over that now.

Kind of.

CRASH.

Another wave sends me toppling back under the water.

AHHHHHHHH!

Cough, cough, cough!

Okay, fine, I'll admit it: I AM AFRAID OF WATER.

Not hot tubs or baths, but oceans, lakes and rivers. Also moats, when I happen to come across them. Basically, I am afraid of bodies of water that have animals in them.

I am also afraid of pools.

They seem shallow but then BOOM the bottom's gone, and you're gulping chlorine.

24

Right now, I need to get out of the ocean, pronto, before it sucks me under for good. As I stand, my pyjamas feel like they weigh two-hundred pounds. My trainers are no longer trainers. They are now bricks attached to my feet.

'I wonder where we are,' Jonah says, swimming up behind me. 'Do you think we're in *Jack and the Beanstalk*?'

Oh! Right! We're in a fairy tale! There must be a fairy tale reason for the water, then. My shoulders relax. 'Do you *see* Jack or a beanstalk?' I ask. There's no ocean in *Jack and the Beanstalk*.

He scrunches up his nose. Hmm, his nose is looking a little red. He might need sunscreen. Crumbs, I don't think I packed any.

Speaking of stuff I packed – where's my suitcase?

I spin around and around until I spot it a few feet away, floating in the other direction. 'Our stuff! We have to get it!'

'I'll get it,' my brother says, diving after it. Except the waves are quick and I can see my red suitcase drifting away faster than Jonah can swim.

'Forget it, Jonah!' I don't want him swimming so far out. It's too dangerous.

'But I don't want to lose my Kadima paddles!' he calls.

'You didn't pack them!' I yell back.

25

'I did when you weren't looking!'

Now I know why my suitcase was so heavy.

Eventually, when the suitcase is nothing more than a red dot in the distance, Jonah gives up and swims back.

Great. Just great. I have nothing to wear but soggy pyjamas and hundred-stone shoes. With a large sigh and a lot of effort, I heave myself onto the dry sand.

SQUISH. When I pull off one of my trainers, a piece of seaweed and a gallon of sandy water spill out.

Jonah is right behind me. 'Abby! I see someone! Is that Jack?' He points to the ocean. In the distance, there's a blob moving toward us.

I squint toward the water. I see a head! A guy's head! But it can't be Jack. Jack climbs; he doesn't swim. Also, Jack is about my age, and this guy looks like a teenager. Wait! Behind the guy's head another head keeps bobbing in and out of the water. A girl's head. At least I think it's a girl's head. I can see long blond hair. They're getting closer...and closer...and... Yup, it's a girl. And then behind her is something green and orange. A towel? A float?

It's shiny and triangle-shaped and reminds me of a paper fan I had as a kid.

Oh! It's a tail! The girl has a tail!

Which can only mean one thing.

'She's a mermaid!' I exclaim. 'We're in *The Little Mermaid*!'

'But who's the mermaid holding?' my brother asks. 'Maybe it's Jack?'

'I am one hundred per cent sure it is not Jack,' I snap.

The guy has dark-brown hair and his eyes are closed. His head is rolling from side to side. That's not a good sign.

I can't tell if this mermaid is *the* Little Mermaid or just a mermaid. I need to remember the original story. My nana read it to me a million times. I just have to focus, and it'll all come back to me. Too bad there's no *time* to focus.

From about twenty feet away, the mermaid's head bobs above the surf. She looks right at us, gasps, and disappears under the water. A second later, she pushes the guy toward us and swims in the other direction.

'We scared her,' Jonah says.

'Wait!' I call to the mermaid. 'Don't leave!'

'I thought we weren't supposed to talk to the people in the story!' Jonah exclaims.

Right. Crumbs.

No time to worry about that now.

The guy is sinking under the surface and it's up to us to save him.

✳ *Chapter Four* ✳

The Real Story

We jump back into the water and each grab one of the guy's arms. He's wearing a yellow shirt and dark-brown trousers that are soaked and torn. He's handsome. Really handsome. Floppy brown hair, chiselled cheekbones. Full lips that are tinged blue.

Uh-oh, that's not a good sign.

'Don't drop him!' I order.

Jonah's eyes are wide with worry. 'Is he okay?'

A wave crashes into my back and I ignore the question. 'Let's just get him to the shore!'

We pull and we heave, and a few minutes later we lie him down on the sand. I cup my ear against his mouth.

He's breathing! 'He's okay! Just unconscious, maybe?'

Jonah exhales in relief. 'Who do you think he is?'

As I collapse on the hot sand beside him, the original story floats back to me. Prince...shipwreck... the Little Mermaid saved the prince... 'Oh! That was the Little Mermaid! And this is the prince she saved from the shipwreck!'

'But why was the prince in the water?'

'Don't you remember?' I ask. Nana read him the same stories she read to me. Although I paid attention 110 per cent of the time and he paid attention about 10 per cent of the time.

He shrugs. 'Just start at the beginning.'

'Fine,' I say. I lie down on the sand and close my eyes, suddenly exhausted. 'There was a mermaid. And she was, um, little.'

'What was her name?' Jonah asks.

Hmm. Good question. 'I don't think she has a name in the actual story.'

'Who wrote the story? Was it the Grimm brothers again?'

'No, it was a Danish guy. Hans Christian Andersen.'

'He liked Danish? The cheese kind?'

I open my eyes just long enough to roll them at my brother and then close them again. 'No, he was from Denmark. The country.'

'But the Little Mermaid lived in the ocean, right?'

'Obviously.'

'Why are you being mean?' he whines.

'Because you're asking silly questions!'

'I'm sorry. I'll stop talking. Just go on with the story.'

'The Little Mermaid really wanted to swim to the surface but she wasn't allowed until her fifteenth birthday. She had lots of older sisters and they'd already done it. When the Little Mermaid was finally allowed to peek out above the water, she saw a prince fall off a boat. Instead of letting him drown, she brought him to shore and saved him.'

'That's what we just saw!' he exclaims.

'Exactly.'

Beside us, the prince coughs up some seawater. Both of us spring up, but the prince's eyes stay closed.

'So what happens next?' Jonah asks.

'Well, after she saved him, she fell in love with him.'

'And then they got married?'

'No,' I say. 'It's kind of a long story, actually, but what happened is that she hid. She didn't want the prince to see her since she was a mermaid. So when he woke up, he didn't know she had saved him. She went back underwater and asked around and discovered that the

30

only way to get a human on land to fall in love with her was to have two legs. And the only way for her to get two legs was to make a deal with the sea witch. So she went to the sea witch and—'

The prince lets out a loud snore.

'And,' I continue, 'the sea witch offered to give her legs, but the witch wanted payment. So the Little Mermaid gave her—' I stop. This part is gross.

'Her pocket money?'

I squirm. 'No.'

'Her trainers?'

'What trainers? She had a tail.'

'Oh. Right. Then what?'

'Her tongue.'

'Are you kidding me?' he gasps. 'The Little Mermaid gave away her tongue?'

I nod, trying not to picture it.

Jonah's eyes light up. 'That's disgusting! Awesome!'

My brother tends to like the gross parts of these stories. He has a stronger stomach than I do. He loves roller coasters. Especially the ones that go upside-down. Not me, thank you very much. I prefer staying upright.

'Well,' I say, 'technically, it was the Little Mermaid's voice that the sea witch wanted. The Little Mermaid had an amazing singing voice. But she gave that up for legs. Forever.'

Jonah shakes his head. 'I can't imagine never speaking again.'

'Me neither,' I say. I doubt you can be a judge if you can't speak. How would you sentence people? 'Also, the sea witch added an extra curse to the spell – if the prince married anyone else, the morning after the wedding, the Little Mermaid would…would…'

'Would what?' Jonah asks. 'Have to give the sea witch her fingers? Her nose?'

'*Snoooort!*' groans the prince, but his eyes stay closed.

'Worse than that,' I say gravely. 'If the prince married anyone else, the morning after the wedding, the Little Mermaid would die.'

Jonah pales. 'But we don't have to worry, right? Because there must have been a happy ending. The prince fell in love with the Little Mermaid, they got married, and they lived happily after?'

'Well…' I hesitate.

Just then we see a splash in the distance. It's the mermaid again. The *Little* Mermaid. Her blonde hair, her green bikini top, and her green-and-orange tail peek out of the water and then disappear.

'I see her,' Jonah whispers. 'Should we hide? Maybe if we run away she'll forget she saw us and the story can continue the way it's supposed to?'

'Yeah,' I say, remembering what I'd said back in the basement. That we should stay out of the way so that whatever fairy tale we landed in wouldn't get messed up.

Except maybe I want to mess this one up.

I look at the Little Mermaid and then back at the prince. 'Here's the thing. The ending of the real story of the Little Mermaid isn't good. It isn't like the happy ending in *Cinderella* or *Snow White*. In the end of the Little Mermaid's real story, the Little Mermaid *doesn't* get the prince. She doesn't get her happy ending at all. In the end of the real story the prince marries someone else, another princess, and the Little Mermaid...' I take a deep breath. 'The Little Mermaid dies.'

'You're wrong,' Jonah tells me. 'I saw the film. The Little Mermaid doesn't die!'

'The movie isn't the real story,' I say. 'Haven't you ever heard of a Hollywood ending? When the film writers give the story a happy ending even though that's not what happens?'

'But she can't die,' Jonah cries, and bangs his fist against the sand. 'That's the worst ending I ever heard!'

I nod. 'It definitely is a bummer.'

Okay. I think I *do* want to mess up the ending. 'I have a new plan. I think we should change the rest of the story.'

He twists his lower lip. 'I thought that was against the rules.'

I throw my hands up in the air. 'Maryrose has never even spoken to us! Whose rules?'

He cocks his head to the side. 'Your rules.'

Oh. Right. 'Yes, well, technically changing the ending is against my rules. But maybe that rule is a mistake. I don't want the Little Mermaid to die. I want to give her a new ending – a happy ending.'

✳ *Chapter Five* ✳

That's What Happened

There's another groan beside me. This time the prince's eyelids flutter.

'I think he's waking up,' my brother says.

The prince's eyes open all the way. He looks at Jonah and then at me. 'Where am I?' he asks, his voice gruff.

'You're on a beach,' Jonah says.

'How did I get here? I was on a ship.' The prince sits up slowly and rubs his forehead. 'I don't remember what happened. Wait. I do remember. There was a storm. I fell overboard. How did I survive?' He notices our soaking wet clothes. 'Did you two save me?'

35

I crouch beside him. 'It wasn't us. It was the Little Mermaid!'

His eyes crinkle. 'The what?'

'The Little Mermaid!' I point to the water. 'She was right there a few minutes ago.'

He twists to look but the water is smooth. 'What's a mermaid?'

'You know,' Jonah says. 'Half fish, half person?'

The prince shakes his floppy hair, and I wonder if he lost his crown in the ocean.

'There's no such thing as a half person, half fish,' he says. 'That's ridiculous.'

'It isn't,' I say. At home, I'd have to agree with him. If one of my new friends told me that she'd seen a mermaid at the beach I would have to ask her if she'd hit her head recently. But we aren't in Smithville. 'Where I live, you'd be right,' I say.

'You don't know that,' Jonah tells me. 'We might have mermaids at home.'

'We do not,' I say.

Jonah shrugs. 'You don't know for sure. He thinks there are no mermaids here and he's wrong.'

Fair point, I guess. I motion around me. 'Where are we, anyway?' I ask. From the beach, I spot a path that leads towards a big stone building in the distance.

Just as I'm trying to figure out what it is, a bell rings from it. A school?

The prince stretches his arms up above his head. 'The kingdom of Mustard.'

Jonah and I both laugh. 'Seriously?' I ask.

The prince squints into the sun. 'Why would I joke about the name of my kingdom?'

'Your kingdom is named after something you put in a sandwich?' Jonah asks.

'Maybe they don't have mustard here,' I say to Jonah. 'Like how in Floom they didn't have brownies.'

The prince shakes his head. 'We eat mustard. It's our favourite condiment. We eat brownies, too. We even dip them in mustard.'

'That's disgusting,' I say.

Even Jonah agrees. 'Yuck,' he says. 'I wish we were in the kingdom of Ketchup.'

My brother is obsessed with ketchup. He puts it on everything. Chips. Mac and cheese. Plain bread.

Seriously, plain bread. Now, that's disgusting.

'Brownies in ketchup,' Jonah says. 'That I'd try.'

Now, that's *really* disgusting.

The prince wobbles to his feet. 'Who are you?' He eyes our outfits. 'You didn't escape from a prison, did you?'

I look down at our matching pjs. Our matching black-

and-white-striped pjs. We do look like convicts.

'No,' I say quickly. 'We're just in our pyjamas.'

'So if you two didn't save me, how did I survive? Maybe a fisherman brought me in? Or I washed up on a piece of driftwood? Or are you two just being modest?'

'No,' I say. 'I can barely swim. It was the Little Mermaid – we just dragged you in.'

'Aha! So you DID save me! Then I, Prince Mortimer, am in your debt. Would you please accompany me back to the palace so you can be celebrated?'

'But Prince Morty…can I call you Prince Morty?' Jonah asks hopefully.

'Only my parents call me Morty.'

Jonah pouts, then continues, 'But Prince Mortimer, it really wasn't us who saved you.'

Hold on. I elbow Jonah in the side.

'Ouch!'

'I just need a minute to talk to my brother,' I say, and yank him a few feet away. 'We may as well go to his palace,' I whisper. 'We might not be able to find the Little Mermaid tonight, and we're going to need somewhere to sleep.'

Jonah shrugs. 'I'm game if you are. But we're definitely going to mess this story up.'

I look out at the water. 'Let's hope so.'

✳ *Chapter Six* ✳

Celebration Time

We're walking up the path towards the building when we run smack into three teenage girls. They all start shrieking the second they see us.

At first I think they're making fun of our matching prison pyjamas, but then I realise they're shrieking at the sight of the prince.

'Oh! My! Goodness!' swoons one.

'It's him! It's him! It's him!' cries another, looking like she might faint.

Jonah and I aren't the only ones dressed in matching outfits – the girls are all wearing white collared shirts, yellow skirts, white knee-socks, and yellow patent-leather shoes. A uniform? I guess the building is a school after all.

'Prince Mortimer!' the third girl cries out. 'Everyone is looking for you! I'm, like, so happy that you're okay!' The girl has a mouth full of bubble gum and super-curly brown hair. Each curl looks like a Slinky.

I wish my curls did that. I also wouldn't mind a piece of gum. Especially since my toothbrush drowned with the rest of my suitcase.

'I'm fine,' the prince says. 'But I need to get back to the palace.'

'Let me get help!' the girl with curly hair says, and then runs back up the path. The rest of the girls just continue to stare.

A few minutes later, she's back with lots of important looking grown-ups, and soon we're on our way to Prince Mortimer's palace.

The hour-long carriage ride swerves us around the beautiful coast. All along the beach are small villas with big outdoor decks and docks and boats. The waves crash against the white sand. The water sparkles like emeralds. The sky is bright blue. Leafy green trees sway in the distance. It kind of looks like the pictures my parents took of their tenth anniversary trip to St Thomas, which is an island in the Caribbean. Even though Nana came to stay with me and Jonah, we were NOT pleased about being left behind. Jonah was bummed to miss out on the Waterinn

Resort's many activities – snorkelling! swimming! kayaking! – while I was bummed that we missed out on the hot tub. Also, I love tall frosty drinks that come with tiny umbrellas, and I'm pretty sure that's what all the drinks are like in the Caribbean.

When we arrive at the palace, there is a crowd of people waiting for us out front. At the centre are the queen and king. They're both wearing gold crowns, but they're not dressed like a typical queen and king. Instead of robes, the king is wearing yellow shorts and a yellow-and-white flowered shirt. The queen is wearing a yellow sundress with a gold belt, gold flip-flops and big gold sunglasses.

These people really like yellow. Oh – it's probably their official colour, since it's the kingdom of Mustard!

Both the king and queen have sun-bleached hair and leathery-looking skin from too many hours spent on the beach. Which is the kind of skin I don't want to have when I'm older. Which is why I always wear sunscreen.

Except for now. Because I didn't realise I'd be going to a beach.

After grabbing the prince in a bear hug, the king turns to us. 'Dudes! We are so grateful that you saved our son,' he says.

Dudes? I'm not a dude. 'It wasn't just us,' I say. 'A

mermaid brought him to shore.'

The king laughs. 'Sure, dude. Whatever you say. We're just grateful that he's okay. After he disappeared off the ship we assumed the worst.'

'You'll be our guests for a few days, won't you, darlings?' the queen asks, not letting go of her son's hand.

'Sure!' Jonah exclaims, gesturing towards the tennis courts to the left of the palace and the volleyball court to the right. 'It's awesome here.'

He's not wrong.

The palace is amazing. All windows and marble. Yellowish marble. These people take the name of their kingdom seriously.

'Darlings, would you like something to drink?' the queen asks. 'Maybe a banana smoothie?'

We nod. That definitely sounds tall and frosty. A minute later a tall, icy yellow drink – with a teeny, tiny yellow umbrella – is plunked into my hand. Hurray!

I slurp it down in twenty seconds. Yum.

Jonah nudges me. 'Not bad, eh, darling?'

I laugh. 'Pretty good, dude, pretty good.'

A maid named Vivian leads us inside the palace. She's about my mum's age, and her brown hair is tied back in a tight bun. She's wearing a perfectly pressed yellow uniform.

Inside the palace, there are yellow flowers everywhere. The rooms are decked out with gold chandeliers and ginormous paintings. Paintings of the ocean, of the king and queen, of the prince, and of other people in crowns.

Vivian leads us upstairs. She opens the door to my room. And by *room*, I mean *suite*. Huge, gorgeous suite.

It's the size of the entire top floor of my house in Smithville. In the middle is a king-sized yellow canopy bed. The room even has a balcony that overlooks the water. From the window I can also see a pool. And a mini-golf course. And a baseball diamond. And a hot tub.

Yes. A hot tub.

Forget the Waterinn – this might be the best hotel ever. Except it's not a hotel. It's Prince Mortimer's house. Our house for the next few days.

Jonah's room is right next door. There's a door between our rooms that connects us if we want to be connected.

'You can unpack here,' Vivian says, motioning to a chest of drawers.

'Thanks,' I say. 'But we lost our luggage. I don't have anything to unpack.'

Speaking of stuff in my suitcase, now that I think about it, I bet the reason Maryrose let us in the mirror right away was *because* I had packed a swimming costume. It's a must-have piece of clothing for this fairy tale. She must not be very happy that I let my suitcase vanish in the ocean.

'Nothing to unpack?' Vivian echoes. 'I'll ring for the royal tailor at once! You absolutely need something for the prince's welcome-home party tonight!'

I can't help but think about that fairy tale, *The Emperor's New Clothes*. Wasn't there a fake tailor who pretended to sew all these new outfits for the emperor, but the emperor was really walking around naked? Hopefully this tailor will make me *actual* clothes.

A few minutes later, the royal tailor knocks on my door to take my measurements. Then he takes Jonah's and hurries away to get to work.

'In the meantime, get in the hot tub and relax,' Vivian orders. 'I'll bring you an extra swimming costume.'

Okay. If she insists.

I slip on the suit – it's yellow with gold, red and green polka dots – and make my way outside in a plush yellow robe and matching slippers.

The hot tub overlooks the ocean. I dip my big toe in first. *Ahhh*. Hot and delicious.

As I sink under the steaming water, I think, *I could get used to this.*

After Jonah – in new yellow swimming trunks – joins me for a bit, we both return to our rooms to get ready.

My wardrobe is now filled with outfits. Real ones – nothing invisible here. There's a beautiful long, flowy yellow dress with a beaded top and a silky skirt. There's also a simpler cotton yellow sundress. Two yellow nighties. A few pairs of yellow undies. I'm going to look very sunny. Good thing they also gave me a new pair of red sunglasses.

I put on the fancy dress and step out onto my balcony, calling to Jonah to meet me outside.

Jonah steps onto his balcony, which is connected to mine with a short divider between them. He's wearing new yellow trousers, a striped yellow-and-white collared shirt, and a massive smile. 'I love it here,' he says. 'This is the best holiday ever!'

'It's not a holiday,' I remind him. But honestly – it does kind of feel like a holiday. The view from here is incredible – blue, blue water that goes on forever. Even though it's warm and sunny, the ocean breeze is gentle and amazing. But still. 'We have a job to do. We *really* have to find the Little Mermaid before it's too late.' I look out into the water, hoping for a glimpse of her. Is she swimming up the coast looking for the prince right now? Where is she?

Jonah pumps his fist in the air. 'We have to stop her from dying!'

'So, here's the plan,' I say, rubbing my hands together. 'We're going to nip this problem in the bud. We're going to stop the Little Mermaid from making the deal with the sea witch in the first place. If she stays a mermaid, then she won't die, even if the prince marries someone else.'

Jonah cocks his head to the side. 'That's not what I think we should do. I think we should let her make the deal with the sea witch and then help her get the prince to fall in love with her so she can live happily ever after.'

What? He can't be serious. 'Jonah,' I say, 'that is the worst plan ever.'

He motions around him. 'But it's so nice here! I bet the Little Mermaid would really like it.'

I wag my finger in his face. 'That is a bad plan for many reasons. First of all, it's very risky. If the Little Mermaid visits the sea witch, then she *has* to get the prince to marry her, or bye-bye mermaid.'

'Everything has risks,' Jonah says. 'We keep going through the mirror even though we never know where we're going to end up or if we can get home. Living on land with the prince is the Little Mermaid's dream. We can't tell her not to dream. Everyone has to dream big, right?'

'Of course we have to dream,' I say, annoyed. 'But if you know your dream is impossible, then you give it up. You find a new dream and you make it work. You get used to it.'

He frowns. 'That's so sad.'

My brother's just not getting it. 'Jonah, we didn't want to move to Smithville, did we?'

He shakes his head. '*You* didn't want to move to Smithville.'

'Fine, *I* didn't want to move to Smithville. But we did and now we're okay. We have friends. We have a magic mirror. It's not so bad. You have to learn to make the best of what you have. You get what you get and you don't get—'

He smirks. 'Wet!'

'Upset,' I say. 'Hmm. Maybe that's the whole point of the original *Little Mermaid* story. That she should have been happy with being a mermaid. The Little Mermaid gave up her whole life – her family, her home, her tail and even her voice – for a guy who didn't appreciate her.'

Jonah nods. 'That's true. She even gave up her tongue.'

'Exactly. If she'd learned to be happy with what she had, she would have been much better off.' I squeeze the railing. 'We have to stop the Little Mermaid from making the biggest mistake of her life.'

He nods. 'You're right.'

Of course I'm right. I'm always right. Well, not always, but usually. 'Now the only issue is – how do we find her?'

'Maybe she'll be at the party?' he asks.

'I doubt she'll be hopping around on her tail,' I say. 'But maybe someone at the party will know how to find her. Before she makes the deal with the sea witch.'

If she hasn't made the deal already.

✳ *Chapter Seven* ✳

Party Hearty

As we hurry down the marble stairs, I glance at my watch, which says it's twelve fifteen at night. Huh? It doesn't feel like it's twelve fifteen. Oh, right, that's the time it is back home.

I look for a clock and see that it's six P.M. here. I guess every hour at home is a day here. We have to be back home by seven A.M., the time Mum and Dad wake us up. So we have six-and-three-quarter hours. Which means six-and-three-quarter days here. That's tons of time to find the Little Mermaid a new happy ending and find our portal home.

As long as my watch is right. We did take a bit of a

swim – I hope this watch is waterproof.

We hear the music from the ballroom and discover that the event is already in full swing. Since we're both starving, we make a beeline for the buffet. Vivian introduces us to Carolyn, the chef, who's setting up the plates of lobster sandwiches, mac and cheese, corn, and, of course, mustard. Lots and lots of mini bowls of mustard.

Carolyn is wearing a poofy yellow chef's hat and a yellow apron. She's about my nana's age.

'Have you guys even tried ketchup?' Jonah asks Carolyn. 'I think you'd like it.'

She makes a sour face. 'Ketchup? Too tomato-y.'

Jonah sighs.

As we munch on the delicious food, we chat with the guests. Everyone wants to meet us, the children who saved the prince.

'It wasn't just us!' I tell anyone who will listen. 'A mermaid was the one to actually save him – we only helped with the last step.'

'A mermaid! What's that, darlings?' asks the queen.

'A half fish, half human,' I explain.

'That's impossible,' the queen laughs. 'You two darlings have fantastic imaginations!'

'Have you ever heard of mermaids?' we ask Vivian as she folds yellow napkins. 'Half fish, half human?'

50

'No such thing,' she snaps.

How are we going to get someone to tell us how to find the Little Mermaid if no one has ever heard of mermaids?

'Psst! Hey!'

Jonah and I turn around to see Carolyn the chef beckoning from a long hallway.

'Does she mean us?' I ask.

'I guess so,' Jonah says. 'Let's go!'

Before I can respond, Jonah has already taken off after her. And of course, I follow. I can't let him chase kind-of strangers by himself.

'I heard your questions and I have something to show you,' Carolyn whispers.

'About mermaids?' I ask.

'Shhhh!' She opens a door that leads to a winding staircase. 'Follow me.'

We take the stairs down a floor until we're in the basement, and then we follow her into a small room.

'You should see this.' In the centre of the room is a small bed covered with a yellow comforter. To the left is a dresser. She opens the bottom drawer and takes out a drawing that's about the size of my hand.

'Look,' she says. 'Careful.'

I take the drawing and realise that it's of a woman

– a woman with a fish tail.

'It's a mermaid!' Jonah exclaims.

'It definitely is,' she says, squaring her shoulders.

'I thought no one here had ever heard of mermaids,' I say.

'They haven't,' she says. 'But I have. My mother gave this drawing to me. She used to tell me stories about the mermaids all the time.'

'Had she seen them?' I ask.

'No,' she says. 'But my great-great-grandmother Edith did. She was lost at sea and a mermaid saved her. She told my great-grandmother about her mermaid friend, who told my grandmother, who told my mother, who told me. I know everything about them.'

'Tell us!' Jonah exclaims.

'They live under the water. In a beautiful kingdom. With streets and houses and restaurants and clothes and everything. The girls are called mermaids and the boys are mermen. And they all have silver tails. And—'

'That's not true,' I interrupt. 'We saw one. She didn't have a silver tail.'

'She must have,' Carolyn huffs. 'That's what my mother told me. And what my grandmother told her. And what—'

'Did your mum say anything about how to get the

mermaids to come on land?' I ask.

'They can't,' Carolyn says. 'Whenever my great-great-grandmother Edith wanted to see her friend, she had to swim into the sea. The mermaid even gave her a potion that let her breathe underwater for twelve hours.'

'Ohhhh,' Jonah's eyes light up. 'Let's take that! Do you know how to make it?'

I shiver. I am not going underwater with or without a potion, thank you very much. There are sharks underwater. Sharks and other animals that want to eat me.

Carolyn nods. 'I do know how to make it, but I can't because one of the ingredients is mermaid spit.'

Gross.

'Find me a mermaid,' she adds, 'and I'll make you the potion.'

Vivian spots us as we return to the party.

'Where have you been?' she asks.

'Just looking around,' I say.

She scowls. 'I hope you're not making a mess for me. Russell! Russell, come here!'

A boy about Jonah's age appears at her side. His skin is suntanned and freckled. Like everyone else in Mustard, he looks like he spends a lot of quality time on the beach.

'This is my son,' Vivian explains. 'He can keep you two company. Russell, why don't you show Abby and Jonah where you play swingball?'

'Let's go sailing instead,' the boy says. 'I think the royal boathouse is still open.'

Yes! That's a great idea. If we're on a boat, we'll be able to find the Little Mermaid. We may not have an underwater potion, but that doesn't mean we can't search the sea.

'No boats!' Vivian snaps. 'It's almost dark, and the sea is too rough.'

Oh well.

'I love swingball,' Jonah says.

Russell nods. 'Let's go!'

'I'm going to stay here,' I say. The last time I played swingball I almost broke my nose.

Tomorrow, we'll take out a boat. Nothing that will tip over. A rowboat maybe. Then we'll find the Little Mermaid. How hard can it be?

✳ *Chapter Eight* ✳

Row, Row, Row Your Rowboat

First thing the next morning, Jonah and I head for the royal boathouse.

We find the yellow hut right on the beach. A tanned guy in mirrored sunglasses is manning the booth. All around him are different kinds of boats. Windsurfers, sailboats, canoes, banana boats.

'We'd like to borrow a rowboat,' I say.

'Of course,' the royal boatman says, handing us a ledger. 'Just sign one out.'

The royal boathouse seems a lot like a library.

'And two life jackets,' I add. 'And do you happen to have some sort of radio? In case the boat drifts off and we need to get in touch?'

The boatman shakes his head.

'Do you have goggles?' my brother asks.

'Yup, those we've got.' He reaches under the counter and hands us two pairs.

'What do we need these for?' I ask my brother.

Jonah scrunches his eyebrows as though the answer is obvious. 'To look underwater for the Little Mermaid.'

'Underwater?' I ask, slightly incredulous. 'Are you crazy? We're not going *in* the water.'

He snorts. 'How else are we going to find her?'

'With our eyes!' I exclaim. 'From the boat!'

'That's just silly,' he says, taking both pairs of goggles and dangling them from his arm. 'We'll swim around.'

My mouth gets super dry. 'We'll see,' I say, but what I really mean is NO WAY.

Jonah turns back to the boatman. 'Do you have snorkels? Or scuba equipment?'

'Are those types of boats?' he asks back.

'I guess not,' Jonah says.

'You don't know how to scuba,' I remind my brother.

My brother shrugs. 'Not yet, but I wanna learn.'

So not happening.

As we make our way to the shore, I see that half the palace is already out on the water. Including the prince, king and queen. All three of them are windsurfing.

'Let's take windsurfers out instead,' Jonah begs, his eyes following them with longing. 'It looks like fun!'

The three royals are being pulled by the wind in all directions. Suddenly, the king flies headfirst into the ocean.

It does not look like fun. It looks terrifying.

'Not a chance,' I snap.

'Enjoy,' the boatman says as we step into the rowboat and sit side by side. He pushes us out into the water, and off we go.

Five minutes later, sweat is dripping down the sides of my face.

The sun is beating on our heads.

'Push! Pull! Push! Pull!' I order.

It turns out that oars are really heavy. Who knew?

The massive yellow life jackets we're both wearing over our swimming things do not help the heat. Between the next push and pull, I catch Jonah trying to take his life jacket off.

'Don't you dare!' I warn.

'But I know how to swim.'

'I don't care. You're my baby brother, and it's my job to make sure you don't drown.'

We push-pull for another ten minutes before I call out, 'Enough.' The water is somewhat calm and we're away from the other boats. Might as well stop here. Also, I'm too tired to go on. My arms feel like rubber. I guzzle water from my canteen and motion for Jonah to do the same. I made sure we both filled up before we left. No getting dehydrated on my watch. Still, I feel like there's something I forgot. But what?

Anyway, it's time to find the Little Mermaid. 'Oh, Little Mermaid!' I call. 'Are you there, Little Mermaid?'

I do not see the Little Mermaid. I just see a lot of blue water.

'We're not going to see her from up here,' Jonah says, putting on one of the pairs of goggles. 'Let's jump in.'

My heart races. 'No, Jonah, that is not the plan.'

'That's my plan,' he says.

'But...but...but...the water has sharks!'

He stands up and looks like he's ready to cannonball in. 'It also has mermaids. And it's not like I'm going to drown. I'm wearing a life jacket.'

He swings his arms back and forth.

'Jonah, you're going to flip the boat!'

'I won't,' he says. And then he hollers, 'Geronimo!' and launches himself over the edge.

Water splashes into my face. 'You're so annoying!' I yell.

He ignores me and waves. 'Come on in! It's so warm!'

What choice do I have now? I can't let him be in the water by himself. What if he needs me? I hug my life jacket to my chest. At least I can't drown with this on.

I can't, right?

Okay. I can do this. My legs shake as I adjust the goggles on my nose. I carefully – very carefully – dip my big toe in. Anything could be hiding underwater. Not just mermaids. But sharks and stingrays and jelly fish and barracudas and crocodiles, and did I mention sharks?

'Just jump!' Jonah yells. 'Don't be such a scaredy-cat!'

My face burns. 'I am not a scaredy-cat!'

'You are, too,' he says. 'You're scared of everything. Sharks. Jumping in the water. Flying by yourself.'

'What are you talking about? I'm not afraid of flying by myself.'

'So why don't you go see Nana on your own this weekend?'

Is he crazy? 'I can't go by myself!'

'Yes you can! My friend Isaac flies by himself once a month. His dad lives in Miami.'

I pause. 'They let a seven-year-old fly by himself?'

'Yup. He's a UM. Unaccompanied Minor. If he

can do it, you can do it.'

Flying by myself does sound a *little* scary. What if I got lost at the airport? What if there was turbulence on the plane? 'Mum would never let me,' I say, my heart hammering.

'It doesn't hurt to ask,' he says. 'Scaredy-cat.'

'I'm not a scaredy-cat!' I snap. And then, before I can change my mind, I jump into the ocean.

I did it! I jumped in! Hurray! Who's a scaredy-cat now, huh? The water is cold. But considering how hot it is outside, it feels good. Really good.

I scream. Something swam by my leg. I take a deep breath. Just a minnow.

I make sure my goggles are on tight, take another deep breath, and peer into the murkiness.

A school of shiny red fish swims by us at top speed. They are very pretty. They are not mermaids.

'Oh, Little Mermaid!' Jonah calls. 'Where are you?'

She does not answer.

We watch as all kinds of fish swim by us. Neon-orange ones. Bright-blue ones. A pink one that looks like a balloon with porcupine needles. Lots of fish, but no mermaids.

'We should head back,' I say eventually. 'This isn't working. We'll have to think of another way.' I help Jonah climb into the boat and then heave myself up behind him.

We both drip water everywhere.

'Where are the towels?' Jonah asks, rubbing his wet arms.

Crumbs. I knew I forgot something.

Dejected, we row our way back to the palace.

'I'm hungry,' Jonah whines.

'We're almost there,' I say. 'You can ask Carolyn to make you a grilled cheese sandwich.'

'I'm not having a grilled cheese sandwich without ketchup. That's just sad.'

That morning Carolyn made us delicious omelettes. And served them with a side of mustard. Jonah had almost started to cry.

'You're crazy,' I say.

'Crazy about ketchup,' Jonah says.

'Can we focus on rowing, please?' I ask. 'The shore is right there! Then I have to figure out a Plan B.'

'Maybe she'll come to us,' Jonah says.

'Push, Jonah, push! Why would she do that?'

'She loves the prince, right? She probably wants to see him.'

'You know,' I say, 'I think you're right. I remember something in the story about her swimming by the shore and trying to get a glimpse of him. Pull, Jonah, pull!'

'I'm pulling,' he snaps. 'More than you're pulling.'

'I guess we'll have to watch the water as much as we can,' I add as the bottom of our boat smashes into the sand.

As we're towing the boat to shore, the queen waves us over to join her for lunch.

'We should change first,' I say.

'Don't be silly,' she says.

So we join the king, queen and prince at the oval table outside for lunch. There's a yellow silk tablecloth, and the dishes and cutlery are all made of gold. I put my yellow silk napkin on my lap like you're supposed to. I elbow Jonah to do the same.

It seems silly to be so formal when we're all in our swimming things, but whatever. The king and prince aren't even wearing tops – they're just in bright-yellow trunks. The queen's swimming costume is pale yellow with a little skirt.

Carolyn serves bowls of squash soup, followed by lemon chicken and yellow rice.

'How was rowing?' the prince asks while chewing a mouthful of rice. For a prince, he doesn't have the best manners. I'd mention it, but you know. He's a prince. He could probably have me beheaded.

'Hard,' I admit. 'We were looking for the Little Mermaid, but we didn't find her.'

'Ha, ha, ha,' they all laugh. 'A mermaid! You two are so funny!'

Sigh.

Carolyn gives me a knowing look as she serves me a bowl of banana sorbet.

After lunch, Jonah and I head to our balconies to try to catch a glimpse of the Little Mermaid from there.

Jonah starts to fidget.

'What's wrong?' I ask.

'We don't *both* have to sit here, do we?'

'Why, do you have other plans?'

He smiles sheepishly. 'I was going to play with Russell. Wanna come?'

'I have to look for the Little Mermaid!'

'Oh,' he says. 'Okay.'

'If you really want to go, you can,' I say, but I don't really expect him to leave me alone.

Jonah jumps up. 'Great! I'll see you later!'

I can't help but feel annoyed. He still thinks this is a holiday! We have work to do.

As I stare at the ocean, I wonder if I'm wasting my time. The water is so busy with all the boats and swimmers. We know the Little Mermaid doesn't want to be seen – so then why would she swim close to the surface during the day? She probably does it at night.

63

I get to my feet. Maybe instead of watching the water, I should spend the day searching the palace grounds for portals to get back home. Make that: *Jonah and I* should spend the day searching the palace grounds.

I find my brother playing ping pong with Russell outside. 'Jonah, I need your help. We have to find the portal home.' I whisper the last part so Russell doesn't hear. I don't know anything about the kid – I'm not going to trust him with our situation yet.

'Let me just finish this game.' Jonah leans over the table and tries to return a shot.

'Jonah! Now!'

'Okay, okay,' he grumbles. 'Sorry, Russell. Wanna come help us knock on all the furniture to find our way home?'

I purse my lips. I guess we're not keeping our situation a secret.

Russell wrinkles his nose. 'Not really. My mum doesn't like it when I touch the furniture.'

I lead Jonah back inside.

'How great is it that Russell gets to live in the palace?' he asks. 'Imagine getting to be here every day.'

'Don't get too comfy,' I say. 'We need to go home eventually. And remember: the portal can be anything. *Any object.*'

We step into the main hallway and Jonah looks around. 'So it could be a – door?' he asks.

I nod. 'Or a mirror. Or a fireplace. Or a table. How are we supposed to know?'

Jonah motions to all the frames on the wall. 'Maybe it's a painting.'

'Maybe,' I say. 'Let's try knocking on them to see if any of them make any sounds or start spinning. But don't let them take you yet, 'kay? Stand back.'

I start with the full-body portrait of Prince Mortimer. He's wearing his crown and a yellow wetsuit. It's really lifelike. His eyes seem to follow me around the room. I knock on the painting three times. It's creepy, but I don't think it's enchanted.

It takes about an hour, but we knock on at least a hundred portraits and paintings.

'Guess it's not the paintings,' I say.

'Are we finished?' Jonah asks eagerly. 'Can I go windsurfing?'

'No, Jonah! We have to check the doors and mirrors.'

We hurry around the palace knocking on all of them. We are almost done when—

'Come in!' Vivian yells when we knock on one of the spare bedroom doors.

Oops. 'Hi,' I say. Inside, I head to the mirror over

the dresser and knock three times.

'What in the world are you doing?' Vivian asks, putting down her duster.

I give a small smile. 'Um, knocking? See, the way we got here was through a mirror, so a mirror might be our portal home.'

'Well, stop it!' she barks. 'You're making the frames uneven. Go and play outside!'

'I agree,' says Jonah.

'Sorry, Vivian,' I say. I pull Jonah back downstairs. We're never going to be able to knock on every object in the house. The palace has a lot of stuff. And Vivian is going to kill us.

'What we need,' Jonah says, sitting down on a marble step, 'is a fairy.'

'This story doesn't have a fairy!' I cry. 'The only magical person in this story is the sea witch, and we can't go and see her since she lives underwater. And I don't happen to have any mermaid spit on me.'

'We should try a bat signal.'

'Huh?'

'You know how in *Batman* they put up a signal in the sky when they need Batman? That's what we need. A bat signal. But in our case, a mermaid signal.'

I'm confused. 'For the sea witch?'

'No, for the Little Mermaid. Something to get her to come faster.'

'But what would draw the Little Mermaid to us?'

'There's only one thing,' Jonah says.

We look at each other and both say it: 'Prince Mortimer.'

* Chapter Nine *

The Prince of Portraits

We try to convince Prince Mortimer to hang out on the beach that night, but he says he's too tired from his day of windsurfing. So we use the next best thing we can find.

Prince Mortimer's wetsuit portrait.

We wait until the middle of the night.

Then we sneak downstairs and very, very, very carefully lift Prince Mortimer's portrait up and off the wall.

'Careful!' I whisper as it leans toward Jonah and almost turns my brother into a pancake.

It's a good thing Vivian lives in the basement with Carolyn and the other staff, or she would definitely hear us right now.

'Got it?' I ask. 'Lift on three and then we'll carry it out. One! Two! Three!'

We lift. But it's so heavy that we end up dragging it across the foyer and out the back terrace to the sand, as close to the water as we can get.

'Do you really think this is going to work?' Jonah asks when we're finally outside.

'Hopefully the Little Mermaid will see this and want to swim right up to it,' I say. 'She *is* madly in love with him.'

'Unless she hates him now that the story's already different,' he says.

'Then all of our problems would be solved,' I say. 'But I doubt it.'

'I just hope she can see it,' Jonah says. 'I could figure out how to build a fire.'

I snort. 'You could not.'

'I could so,' he huffs. 'You just need the sun and a piece of glass. How hard could it be?'

'Hard, considering it's the middle of the night.'

'Oh, right.'

Luckily it's a full moon, so we don't need to rely on

my brother's nonexistent fire-starting skills. Everything on the beach is lit up. Including the portrait. Including the water lapping at the base of the portrait. Wetting the paint.

'Quick! Jonah! The prince is losing his feet!'

We hurry to move the portrait back a few feet. I doubt we'd be the royal family's welcome guests if we ruined one of their prized paintings.

'So, what now?' Jonah asks.

'We wait. She'll see the portrait and swim up to us and we'll talk to her. I'll sit behind the painting and hold it up while you keep watch.'

At least an hour passes. Jonah's eyes are drooping.

Another hour.

Jonah's eyes are closed.

'Jonah, wake up!' I yell. 'I can't do both jobs at once!'

'Not sleeping!' he announces and opens his eyes wide.

'Let's switch,' I say. 'That way you can pretend not to sleep while you balance the portrait, and I'll look for her.'

We switch. Jonah dozes. I scoop sand from one hand to the other, keeping watch.

When I feel my own eyes start to droop, I decide it's time to call it quits. This is getting us nowhere. I'll give it ten more minutes, and then we're going to—

Splash.

Did I just hear that? Or is it my imagination? I spring to my feet and run closer to the shore.

I see her! I see her! Long green-and-orange tail. Really gorgeous blonde hair. It goes down to her waist and is almost the colour of butter.

She's treading water by a rock, gazing at the wetsuit portrait of Prince Mortimer.

I want to yell, 'Hello!' but I'm afraid of startling her and sending her back under the water. She's not too far out – maybe twenty feet. The water is calm.

If only I could swim out twenty feet. If only I had on a life jacket.

Maybe I can swim out a little. Not too deep. Just to where I can still stand.

Luckily I'm wearing my swimming costume under my sundress. I slip off the dress and wade into the water. Slowly. Carefully. Without making a sound. Without making a splash. Wow, the water is cold at night. I wish *I* had a wetsuit.

I almost reach her when the water hits my waist. That's as far as I'm going to go.

'Abby?' Jonah's voice echoes along the beach. 'Where are you?'

Uh-oh.

Jonah stands up on the shore, still holding the painting.

71

'Abby!' he yells, blinking the sleep from his eyes. 'Where did you go?'

I want to yell, 'SHHHH,' but I don't want to scare the Little Mermaid.

'Abby! Abby!'

The Little Mermaid sinks her shoulders and tail under the surface.

'Wait!' I cry. 'Little Mermaid! Please don't go! We want to help you!'

She disappears under the water.

I lunge toward her. 'No! Don't go! We know you love the prince! That's why we brought his painting! To get your attention!' Suddenly my feet no longer touch the ground. Oh, no.

'Abby!' Jonah hollers. 'I see her! She's in the water.'

'No kidding, Jonah! Can you lend me a hand here, please?'

'You're the girl from the other day, right?' a voice asks timidly. The Little Mermaid! She's talking to me!

'I am,' I say, frantically doggy-paddling to stay afloat. 'Don't be afraid. We want to help you.'

Her face peeks out from behind the rock. 'Is that your brother?'

'He definitely is,' I say, finally finding the sand with my tiptoes. 'You only have sisters, right?'

72

She nods.

'Lucky.' I laugh. 'And you're the youngest, huh?'

She nods again and runs her fingers through her wet hair. 'How did you know that?' she asks. 'Humans never know anything about me.'

'Yeah, well, I've read your story. That's what I want to talk to you about. I know that you're a mermaid and that you love the prince and that you want to trade your tail for two legs.'

She gasps. 'I haven't told anyone that.'

'I read it. In a book.'

'You know how to read?'

My eyes widen. 'You don't?'

Splash. I turn to see Jonah swimming toward us.

The Little Mermaid shakes her head. 'No one underwater does. Books and ink don't last underwater. They disintegrate.'

That makes sense. 'Well, we read. And that's how we know who you are. And what happens to you. And it isn't good.'

She pulls on a lock of her hair. 'What happens?'

'You go to the sea witch and make a deal with her. She turns your tail into two legs but makes you give her your voice as payment.'

She touches her throat. 'My voice?'

73

I nod.

'Your tongue!' Jonah adds, now beside us.

'That's disgusting,' the Little Mermaid says.

I agree. 'That's why we don't want you to do it.'

'Is your name really Little Mermaid?' Jonah asks.

She shakes her head. 'It's Lana.'

'I'm Jonah,' my brother says. 'And my sister is Abby.'

'Nice to meet you, Abby and Jonah. I've never spoken to humans before.'

'We've never spoken to a mermaid before,' Jonah says. 'Most people here haven't even heard of mermaids. They're weird. They don't use ketchup, either. Is there ketchup where you live?'

It's very late, I'm very cold, and I do not feel like chatting about ketchup. 'Lana, let's get back to business. Are we all clear? You can't trade your voice and tail for legs to make Prince Mortimer fall in love with you. It doesn't work. He marries someone else and you end up...' My voice trails off. A wave hits me and I struggle to steady myself.

Lana squints. 'I end up what?'

'Dead,' Jonah says matter-of-factly.

She shivers. 'I don't want to be dead.'

'Exactly,' I agree. 'That's why you have to learn to be happy with your life in the water. You get what

74

you get and you don't get upset.'

In the moonlight, I see Lana's eyes tear up. 'But I don't want to stay where I am! I love Prince Mortimer! And I want to live on land! Where there are sunsets and flying fish!'

'What are flying fish?' Jonah asks.

'You know,' she says. 'Fish that fly through the air. My sisters told me all about them!'

'You mean birds?' I wonder.

'Flying fish!' she insists. 'And shoops!'

'What are shoops?'

'The things you put on your feet. You know – shoops.'

'You mean shoes,' Jonah says.

She shakes her head. 'Shoops!'

'Forget about shoops,' I say. 'Didn't you hear what I said? You're going to lose everything! Your tongue! Your life! You can't make a deal with the sea witch! You can't give up everything that makes you who you are. It's just not right.'

Lana crosses her arms and pouts. Her tail slaps against the water. I guess that's her way of stomping her feet. 'But I love him.'

She's being ridiculous. 'You've never even spoken to him!'

'You don't need to speak to someone to know you

love him,' she insists. 'You don't know what it's like. You're just a kid.'

I snort. 'You're practically a kid, too.'

'I'm fifteen,' she huffs.

'That's not even old enough to vote!'

'Vote on what?' she asks.

'The president,' I say.

'We don't have presidents here. My father is the king. He runs the ocean. And I'm a princess. And I want to marry the prince.'

Jonah floats on his back. 'Maybe she could still marry the prince, without making a deal with the sea witch. Maybe they can have a long-distance relationship. Or maybe she can live in the pool. Or he can go live with her in the ocean. He can use the underwater spit potion!'

Lana cocks her head to the side. 'There's an underwater spit potion?'

'That's what Carolyn said,' I say. 'But she hasn't been right about everything. She's the chef at the palace. Apparently her great-great-grandmother met a mermaid.'

'I've never heard of a potion,' Lana says, 'but if it really worked, then the prince could stay with me!'

'Carolyn said it lasted only for twelve hours,' Jonah says. 'So he'd have to come back on land eventually.'

'Maybe we could alternate,' Lana says hopefully. 'He

could spend some time underwater with me, I'll spend some time in his pool...'

'It's doable,' I say.

'But...' Lana hesitates. 'Do you think he'll love me even if I'm a mermaid?'

'A guy should love you for who you are,' I say. 'If you have to change yourself, he's not right for you.'

We all nod. Sounds right, doesn't it?

'I like the potion-plus-pool plan,' I say. 'That way you can still be together without trading anything with the sea witch. I think the prince has to meet you. Once he sees that you're real, and once you tell him that you're the one who saved him from the shipwreck, I'm sure he'll fall in love with you.'

'Yeah?' Lana asks.

'Absolutely,' I say, and hope that it's true.

✳ *Chapter Ten* ✳

The Ocean Can't Hide Everything

The next morning, Jonah, Prince Mortimer and I head out to the beach, as planned.

'Is she really going to be here?' Prince Mortimer asks.

'Yup. She can't wait to see you again,' I say.

Jonah and I told him that the person who swam him to shore is here to see him. We left out the mermaid part, since he didn't believe us the first time we told him. He'll find out the truth soon enough.

My plan is totally going to work. He's going to meet Lana and fall hopelessly in love. So what if she's a mermaid? That won't stop true love! In a few weeks, he'll propose, they'll get married, and – *ta-da!* – happy ending. I glance at my watch. It's only two o'clock back home. We'll get Lana and Prince Mortimer together, and we'll still have five days to find our way back!

We are really getting good at this fairy tale stuff.

As we walk down to the shore, I spot Lana already waiting in the ocean. Her upper body is above the water and her tail is underneath. From this angle, you can't even tell she's a mermaid.

Prince Mortimer's eyes light up. 'That's her?'

'Yup,' I say.

'She's beautiful.' He practically skips all the way down to the water. 'Hello!'

She smiles back. 'Hello!'

'Are you really the one who saved me from the shipwreck?' he asks.

She nods. 'I did. I brought you to Crescent Beach, and then Abby and Jonah pulled you ashore.'

'I am forever in your debt,' he says, tipping his head. 'Come out of the water so we can talk.'

'It's so hot out,' she says, blushing. 'Why don't you come in the water?'

Nice one, Lana!

'I don't have my swimming trunks on yet,' he says. 'Tell me more about how you saved me. You happened to be in the water that night?'

'Yes,' she says simply.

'I guess you were on another boat?'

She smiles. 'Something like that.'

'You have beautiful hair.'

'Thank you,' she says, batting her eyelashes.

'So you brought me all the way to safety?'

She nods.

His eyes are all shiny and moony. 'That's amazing. You saved me, and you're so beautiful.'

'Thanks again,' she says.

He clears his throat. 'Will you marry me?'

Wow, that was fast! I thought it would take a few weeks, but it only took a few minutes. Maybe it really is true love!

Lana's smile lights up her face. 'I will!'

'Fantastic,' he says, his eyes twinkling. 'You will be my princess.'

'I should tell you something,' she says. 'I am already a princess.'

Surprise crosses his face. 'You are? Princess of where?'

'Of the sea,' she says, and with that she dives into the water and shows him her tail.

His face turns white.

Uh-oh.

She reemerges, still smiling.

'You have a t-t-tail!' he spits out.

'I do,' she agrees. 'I'm a mermaid.'

He shakes his head repeatedly. 'There is no such thing as mermaids.'

Jonah laughs. 'Prince Mortimer, she has a tail. You can't argue with that.'

The prince waves his hands in front of his face and takes a few steps back. 'I can't marry a half person, half fish.'

What? No! 'Why not?' I ask. 'She can sleep in your pool! Or the hot tub! The hot tub is really relaxing!'

He keeps walking back toward his palace. 'I just can't! I need a wife who can walk and dance. Someone who can live with me on land. I'm sorry, but this will never work. I take back my proposal!'

'You can't take back a proposal!' I yell.

'Yeah!' Jonah hollers. 'Finder's keepers!'

'There's a potion,' I tell him. 'A potion you can take. You'll be able to live part-time with her under the water.'

'There are sharks under the water!' he exclaims. 'And I'm not giving up my palace to live in some underwater cave!'

Hmph. What a romantic.

And with that, he turns and storms back to the palace.

'But, but, but…' Lana's voice trails off. 'I don't live in a cave. My father's palace is just as nice as this palace.'

I hurry towards her. 'Lana, I'm so sorry.'

She winces. 'I told you this wouldn't work. I need legs to marry him. And the only way to get them is the sea witch.'

'Lana, I don't get it. Why are you so crazy about him? He just insulted your palace! And he's not willing to give anything up for you! Why are you going to give everything up for him?'

She purses her lips. 'Because I love him!'

I roll my eyes. I can't help it. She's hopeless. 'There has to be another way.' I rub my fingers against my temples. 'I need to think about it.'

'Well, I need legs. I have to go, anyway. My dad is having a party tonight and I said I'd be there.'

'Good.' At least a party will keep her from visiting the sea witch. 'By tomorrow I'll have another plan. Trust me, I'm very good at planning.'

Jonah nods. 'She is very good at planning.'

'Just whatever you do, don't go to the sea witch. Deal?' I ask.

'Whatever,' she says. And then, without even a goodbye, she disappears under the water, leaving me to come up with another plan. Fast.

∗ *Chapter Eleven* ∗

That Hurts

Once again, I toss and turn and turn and toss. I can't sleep. Lana is going to come by in the morning, and I have no idea how to get her a happy ending. My only option is to convince her that her current life is super awesome *without* the prince.

And it *so* is. She's a princess! She has great hair! If she lived where we do, she could be in a shampoo advert. She has five sisters – I wish I had *one* sister, never mind five. Legs just aren't *that* great. I look down at mine. Sure, they can run and dance and stuff. But I've seen her swim, and she moves a lot faster than I do.

There's a loud noise outside the window. It sounds

like, 'Oooooh!' but it's more of a moaning.

I bet it's quieter underwater. Land has all kinds of creepy sounds.

'Ooooh!' I hear again.

Wait. That sounds like a person.

I run out to the balcony and look down at the beach.

'Ooooooooh!' I hear a third time. I look around in the moonlight and eventually see that the sound *is* coming from a person. From Lana. She's lying on the sand.

As I try to figure out what's going on, she starts to flop from side to side. Her tail starts to quiver. And then as I watch, her tail splits right down the middle into two.

OH. MY. GOODNESS.

I have seen a lot of crazy things in fairy tale worlds. But I have never seen anything like this.

I step over the divider and pound on Jonah's balcony door. 'Wake up!' I yell. 'We have to help her!'

When I turn back to Lana, the green in her legs is slowly fading to the same light colour of her skin. Her hair is the same. Her upper body is the same. But now she has legs. LEGS!

And green bikini bottoms.

'What's up?' Jonah asks, opening his balcony door.

'That's what's up!' I say, pointing to Lana. 'She made the deal with the sea witch! Why would she do that when I told her not to?' I stomp my right foot. I am cross. So very cross.

'Oooohhhh!' Lana moans.

'We need to help her,' I say. 'Get a towel.'

We hurry down to the beach and find her still twisting in pain on the sand.

'Does it hurt?' Jonah asks her.

'Obviously, it hurts!' I exclaim. 'She wouldn't be making those sad sounds if it didn't hurt!'

Lana just nods.

I put my hands on my hips. 'Did you go to the sea witch?'

She nods again.

'Why would you do that?' I wonder aloud. 'I told you *not* to!'

She opens her mouth to say something but then immediately closes it.

I gasp in horror. Since she has legs and went to the sea witch...the sea witch has her...has her...has her tongue. 'Did you give her your...?' I can't even say the word. It's too gross.

Lana nods. But then she points to her legs.

My stomach churns. She really did it. Gave away her tongue for legs. Why would she do that? Why would anyone do that?

I take a deep breath. I take the towel from a very wide-eyed Jonah and wrap it around her wet shoulders. 'Can you stand?' I ask.

She shrugs, which I take to mean *I don't know*. Communicating with someone with no tongue is *not* going to be easy. She holds my hands, and I gently lift her up.

She's shaky on her feet, but it seems to work. At the same time, she grimaces, so I guess it hurts. After a few seconds, she is able to walk on her own.

We take her back to the palace.

I want to yell at her. To tell her that she made a huge mistake.

But by the pained look on her face, I think she already knows it.

'Come and sleep in my suite,' I tell her. 'We'll deal with this in the morning.'

She looks like she wants to say something, but then just nods. Without a word, she follows me to my room.

✳ *Chapter Twelve* ✳

Nice to Meet You Again

Lana is up before I am. She's sitting on the floor of my room, examining her toes.

'How are you feeling?' I ask.

She gives me a big smile and a thumbs-up.

She motions to her body. I have no idea what she's trying to say.

She motions again.

'You're cold?'

She shakes her head.

'Hot?'

She tugs on the yellow nightie I lent her last night. Maybe she's saying thank you.

'You're welcome,' I tell her.

She shakes her head again and then makes a waving motion with her hands.

'You want to go swimming?'

Her cheeks turn red and she stomps her foot. She pulls at the nightie again and grunts.

'Oh, you want to get dressed!'

She gives me a big nod. Then she makes a show of patting down her hair.

'You want to wash your hair and then get dressed and then see Prince Mortimer?'

She claps. I guess I got it.

The door bursts open. 'Who are you?' Vivian looks at Lana and demands.

Lana's eyes widen in fear. She opens her mouth to answer but then seems to remember she can't say anything.

'She's a mermaid!' I say. 'Remember I told you I was looking for a half fish, half human?'

Vivian clucks her tongue. 'She doesn't look like she's half fish. She has legs.'

Good point. 'Well, she used to be half fish,' I say.

'I don't approve of lying, Miss Abby,' Vivian says. 'Does your friend with legs have any clothes, or did she lose her luggage, too?'

I shake my head. 'No luggage.'

'I'll call the tailor,' Vivian barks.

Twenty minutes later, Lana has been measured and has showered and is wearing a brand-new sleeveless yellow sundress. She still smells a little salty, but I guess that's what happens when you live most of your life in the ocean.

'Now get outside, both of you, so I can clean,' Vivian orders.

Through the balcony window, we spot Prince Mortimer already out on the beach, standing by the royal boathouse. Jonah is up, too – he and Russell are building sandcastles.

Prince Mortimer looks up and Lana waves at him.

Prince Mortimer waves back and gives Lana a slightly quizzical look.

Lana curtsies. Then she pulls my hand and hurries me outside.

Prince Mortimer watches us as we approach.

'Hi,' I say. 'Do you remember Lana? She gave up her tail to be with you, so I hope you're happy.' I don't mean to sound as grumpy as I do, but I guess I can't help it. I feel grumpy.

'You have legs!' the prince exclaims.

She blushes and nods.

'She gave up her voice for those legs,' I say.

Lana gives me a sour look.

What? She did! Lana should be thanking me. In the

89

original story, the Little Mermaid had no translator, and the prince never knew that she was the one who saved him and he ended up marrying someone else. The only reason he knows what's going on here is because of me.

And maybe Jonah. My brother who is currently making snow angels in the sand.

Mostly me.

'Who cares about your voice?' the prince exclaims. 'You look gorgeous.'

I have no choice but to roll my eyes.

He takes Lana's hand and twirls her around. Then he drops to one knee. 'I will honour my earlier proposal. Will you marry me?'

She nods happily.

Lana and the prince embrace. Everyone on the beach – the king, queen, Jonah, Russell and the guy manning the royal boathouse – claps and cheers.

And me? Honestly, I'm not sure how I feel. On the one hand, I'm happy that Lana got what she wanted. She wanted to marry the prince and now she will. She's getting her happy ending.

But on the other hand, she:

1. Lost her tail!
2. Lost her voice!

3. Lost her underwater kingdom! Will she ever even see her family again?
4. Is marrying a guy who only likes her for her legs!

Even though she seems happy, I can't help feeling sad.

The prince takes Lana's hand. 'We'll get married immediately. Three days from now. We'll do it in the ballroom, of course.'

Of course? I had so expected him to stay on the beach.

Lana follows him into the palace. For someone who just got legs, she looks very glamorous as she walks.

'See?' Jonah says, running up to me, covered in sand. 'It all worked out.'

'Not all of it,' I say. I can't shake the sad feeling.

'So now what?'

'I guess we go home.'

'Already?' He looks longingly at the water. 'Don't you think we should stay a few more days? Just until the wedding? That way we can make sure Lana gets married and has her happy ending. What time is it at home?'

I glance at my watch. 'Three A.M.'

'Great!' he cheers. 'Then we have four hours until Mum and Dad wake us up. Which is four days. I'm going kayaking.'

I grab his arm before he runs away. 'We need

to look for the portal!'

'We will, we will,' he says. 'How about we split up?

'All right,' I say. 'That sounds reasonable.'

He scrunches his nose. 'You go and check the furniture,' he says.

'We already checked the mirrors. I guess I can check the tables and chairs. What are you checking?' I'm glad he's finally willing to do some work.

As he runs toward the beach, he calls over his shoulder, 'I'm going to check all the kayaks!'

I walked right into that one.

* *Chapter Thirteen* *

Lost in Translation

The next day, we're in the dining room having tea and discussing wedding details.

Chef Carolyn can't stop staring at Lana. 'She's really a mermaid?' she asks, eyes wide.

'She was, but she gave it up,' I explain.

'I wish she could talk! I have so many questions!'

The prince clears his throat. 'Back to the menu,' he says. 'Chef Carolyn, I'd like you to prepare sole, tilapia and yellowfin tuna. Fish, in honour of my little mermaid!'

Lana's eyes widen to the size of her teacup.

'What's wrong, my pet?' Prince Mortimer asks, patting her knee. 'You don't like tuna?'

She shakes her head frantically.

'What about sole?'

More head shaking.

'Then what would you like to serve?' he asks.

She shakes her head no, and then makes a weird squiggly motion with her hands.

'She doesn't want fish. She must want lobster. Perfect!' He kisses her on the forehead, gets up and leaves the room.

Lana's eyes fill with tears.

'Did you not want lobster?' I ask.

She shakes her head.

'Wait, I'm confused,' Jonah says. 'You did want lobster or you didn't?'

She shakes her head again.

'Which one?'

Lana drops her head down on the table and sighs.

What can I say? It's tough to talk without a voice.

Since they got engaged, the prince and Lana don't seem to understand each other at all. Lana does a lot of nodding and shaking her head, but it's tough to answer questions like: What do you want to serve for dinner? You can't answer that with a nod or a head shake.

Vivian hurries into the living room clutching a paper card. 'Look,' she calls out. 'The calligrapher just finished the wedding invitations. Don't they look nice?' She places one in Lana's hands. 'I'll send one to your family.'

Lana shakes her head. I notice that her eyes fill with tears but that she blinks them away.

'You're not inviting your dad?' I ask, shocked.

She shakes her head again.

Communicating would be so much easier if mermaids knew how to read and write.

'What about your sisters?' I ask. 'Aren't they going to be your bridesmaids?'

She points to me.

'Me?' I ask. 'You want me to be your bridesmaid?'

She nods.

Wow! I've never been a bridesmaid before. But I've always, always, ALWAYS wanted to! The dress! The bouquet! I don't know what else bridesmaids do, but I'm sure it's fun.

'I accept!' I cheer. 'I'm going to be an amazing bridesmaid. The best bridesmaid ever. But wait – if I'm the only bridesmaid, does that make me the maid of honour?'

Lana nods.

This is the most exciting thing that has ever happened to me. Besides falling into fairy tales through my magical mirror, obviously.

I am going to be *the* Little Mermaid's maid of honour! Who else can say that? No one! Only me! 'But are you sure you don't want to ask your sisters?'

She shakes her head and looks down at the invitation.

'Read it out loud!' Jonah says.

I shoot him a look across the table.

He blushes. 'Oh, right. I keep forgetting you can't talk.'

'She can't read, either,' I say. A lightbulb goes off in my head. 'I have an idea! An idea that's going to fix everything. Okay, not everything, but definitely your communication problems.'

Lana looks up at me eagerly.

I wait for Jonah to make a drum roll or something, but when none comes I turn to Lana and announce, 'I'm going to teach you to write! If you can write, then you'll be able to communicate with Prince Mortimer. And with everyone. Then you won't be so frustrated. When anyone asks you a question you can just write the answer down!'

'Great idea, Abby,' Jonah says. 'I think I'll go and play tennis while you do that. Russell is having his tutoring lessons now, but maybe I can get him to sneak away.'

I sigh.

Lana points to the invitation.

I don't understand what she wants. 'You want me to read it to you?'

She shakes her head no. She nods. She shakes her head

96

no again. She points to herself and then her eyes and then the invitation.

'I think she wants you to teach her to *read*, too,' Jonah says.

'Of course! Reading and writing go hand in hand.' I square my shoulders. 'Just call me Professor Abby.' All I need now is a pair of glasses and a blazer. Oh, and pencils. And paper. 'Jonah, before you disappear for the day, please find me some paper and pencils.'

Jonah hurries off. When he comes back with paper and different-coloured pencils, I spread them all out on the table.

Pencils, check! Paper, check!

Now what? I've never actually taught anyone to read before. Where do I start?

'Okay, bye!' Jonah calls.

'Wait! Jonah. You learned to read more recently than me, right?'

'Right,' he says.

'Can you, um, tell me how to start?'

He fidgets with the door. 'How about with A?'

I nod. 'So we'll go through all the letters, and I'll teach Lana the sounds. Thanks. You can go now.'

Jonah bolts out the door.

I write a capital A. No need to confuse her with small

letters yet. 'A makes an "ahhhh" sound. Ahhh!' I overemphasise. 'Also, sometimes "ay". A is for... "Abby"! That's me. A is also for "at" and "animal". Why don't I write it down and then you copy it?'

I write a big A, and then she copies it ten times.

I smile. 'A is for "awesome". Now let's do B. Do you know what B is for?'

She shakes her head.

'B is for "brother",' I say. 'And "ballroom". And best of all, "bridesmaid".'

✳ *Chapter Fourteen* ✳

Read It and Weep

L ana is a fast learner. By the end of the day, she knows the whole alphabet. By the day before the wedding, she can pretty much read and write.

It helps that we recruit Russell's tutor. I'll admit it: I'm no reading and writing expert. But it was all my idea, so I'm taking credit for it anyway, thank you very much.

Lana decides not to tell Prince Mortimer what she's up to. She wants it to be a surprise. Since he's always outside surfing, canoeing, or windsurfing, it hasn't been much of a problem.

When Lana takes breaks, we are very busy with

wedding prep. We go to dress fittings with the palace tailor. Lana's dress is the perfect bride's dress – white, strapless and fitted on top, with a big, poofy skirt. My maid-of-honour dress has capped sleeves, a sweetheart neckline and a short skirt. It's pretty gorgeous – and yellow, of course.

Also, as maid of honour, it is my job to help Lana prepare for her big march down the aisle. I make her practise walking. Heel-toe, heel-toe, heel-toe. I read a book about a model once, and that's how she was told to walk down the catwalk. I'm guessing it's the same for a wedding.

I even practise my own walking – as maid of honour I have to make sure not to trip.

Being maid of honour is pretty important, you know. And time-consuming.

My job is to keep Lana happy and worry-free all day. Also to get an updo, manicure and pedicure on the morning of the wedding. Yup, the bride and the maid of honour both get their hair and nails done! I've never had an updo, manicure, or pedicure, so I'm thrilled.

Now, the day before the wedding, while Lana studies with Russell's tutor, I try to find the portal home. I knock on everything I see. Bedposts. Bowls. Stairs. Nothing works.

Jonah is supposed to be helping, but he's too busy holidaying.

'Can you please help me?' I ask him, finding him doing handstands in the pool.

'Abby, I'm sure it will be something at the wedding. The portal usually pops up at the *end* of our adventure.'

'Jonah, of course it pops up at the end of our adventure! Once we find it, we leave!'

'Not true,' he says, floating on his back. 'We wait until the happy ending is all straightened out and then we leave. The happy ending here isn't all straightened out yet.'

'It practically is,' I tell him.

'Then I'm sure we'll figure it out tomorrow,' he says. 'Why don't you come swimming?'

'Just because you're taking a break doesn't mean I can,' I huff. Although it is very hot. And the pool does look very refreshing. But also deep. Anyway, I have other things to do.

I leave my brother to feel guilty in the pool while I go to check on Lana.

She's scribbling on a piece of paper. She's writing! My plan totally worked!

'What are you writing?' I ask.

She takes a clean piece of paper and writes, 'RITING PRESINT FOR PRINS.'

Okay, so she's not the best speller yet, but come on. Two days ago she didn't even know that her name started with the letter L. Give her a break.

'Cool,' I say.

She nods. Her cheeks are flushed with happiness.

'What is it?'

She points her pencil at her notebook.

It says:

'ONCE UPON A TIME THER WAS A MERMAD PRINCES. ON HER 15 BIRTHDA SHE SAW A PRINS FAL IN THE WATER—'

'Oh!' I squeal. 'It's the story of how you met!'

She nods.

'He's going to be so impressed,' I say. 'Wait, Lana, I want to ask you a question. How come you don't want to invite your family to the wedding?'

She sighs. She pulls out a fresh piece of paper and writes, 'THEY CANT COM ON LAND. AND THEY MUST BE VERE CROS WIV ME. AND NOT FEEL LIKE CELEBRATING.'

'Are you sure? We could send them the invite – you never know what they might say.'

'NO,' she writes. 'THEY CANT REED.'

Oh, right.

That's so sad! She seems to think so, too, because I

catch her frowning and gazing towards the window that overlooks the water.

On the bright side: I'm still the maid of honour!

✳ *Chapter Fifteen* ✳

Your Bed Has Been Made

That night we all eat together in the dining room.

It's a pretty delicious dinner. Chef Carolyn makes a barbeque. There are cheeseburgers and corn and grilled salami. Of course, there's mustard. For dessert we have banana pie and lemon cake. These people really know how to eat, even if most of the food is yellow.

During dessert, Lana stands up and hands a box to Prince Mortimer. There's a yellow ribbon tying it closed.

'What's this?' he asks.

She smiles.

'It's her wedding gift to you,' I explain, not wanting to

give away the surprise but bursting with excitement. How amazing is she that she learned to write in two days? She's amazing! And it was all my idea! I am the best maid of honour ever!

Prince Mortimer unwraps the ribbon, opens the box, and takes out pretty papers laced together with ribbon. The first page reads: *Our Story, by Princess Lana.*

'How nice,' the prince says before placing it beside his plate. He goes right back to his lemon cake.

Lana looks shocked.

I *feel* shocked. 'Aren't you going to read it?'

'I'm in the middle of dessert,' he explains, taking another forkful. 'Yum.'

Lana's face falls.

No. No, no, no. 'But don't you see what a big deal this is? Lana wrote that! Herself! She learned to read and write so you guys can communicate!'

Prince Mortimer takes a big gulp of pineapple juice before continuing. 'What does Lana need to read and write for? She's a princess. She just needs to smile, dance and be beautiful.'

I drop my fork and it clatters against my plate.

Jonah's jaw drops open.

Lana gasps. She looks at Prince Mortimer and then back at me. She shakes her head. Then she pushes her chair back and runs out of the room.

Everyone else at the table shrugs.

'Guess she doesn't like lemon cake,' the prince says, and continues eating. 'You know what we should have at the wedding? Lemon meringue pie.'

I can't listen to one more minute of this. I excuse myself from the table and hurry after Lana. I do kind of hope they have lemon meringue pie at the wedding, though. I love lemon meringue pie.

When I walk into her room, just down the hall from mine, she is pacing.

'Sorry about that,' I say.

Lana throws her arms up in the air. She picks up a paper and pen and writes, 'I THINK I MAD A BIG MISTAK!!!'

I think she made a big mistake, too. Which I told her from the beginning. Not that I'm going to say, 'I told you so,' now. Even though I really want to.

But I won't.

Her eyes tear up, and she continues writing:

'I GAVE UP EVERETHING TO BE HERE. MY FAMILIE. MY HOME. MY VOICE. MY SISTERS!! MY DAD! OH MY POOR DAD.'

'What's wrong with your dad?' I ask. 'Isn't he the king?'

106

She nods. 'HE IS LONELLY SINCE MY MUM DIED 10 YEARS AGO.'

Her poor dad. First he lost his wife, and now he has pretty much lost his daughter. I sit down on her perfectly made bed. I'm impressed. She makes a good bed.

'WHAT SHUD I DO?'

As I glance down at the bed, I remember one of my mum's favourite expressions. 'You made your bed, and now you have to sleep in it,' I say.

She shakes her head and then writes, 'VIVIAN MADE MY BED!'

Oh. Right. She probably made Jonah's, too. I, on the other hand, made my own bed, thank you very much. Anyway, that's not the point. 'It's an expression,' I say. 'What I mean is, I'm not sure what you *can* do except get married.' And this isn't because of the maid of honour thing. I swear. 'You can't go back to your family. You don't have a tail. Can you swim in the ocean the way you are now?'

She shakes her head no.

'And, anyway, if you cancel the wedding, he'll marry someone else. And then...' my voice trails off.

And then.

Although maybe the deal with the sea witch changed. It's possible, isn't it? Since the story has changed? 'Did the sea witch tell you that if the prince marries someone else you'll...you'll...stop living the next morning?' I can't bear to say the word die.

She nods.

Crumbs.

We can't let that happen. No matter what.

✶ *Chapter Sixteen* ✶

On the Other Hand

It's W-day. Wedding day.

And M-day: Maid-of-honour Day.

Also, G-day: Go-home Day. Assuming we can find the portal. My watch says it's just before six, so technically we have until tomorrow, but I don't want to be late.

I spend the morning in the royal salon getting ready. When they wash my hair with yummy lemon-scented shampoo and conditioner, I lean back and admire the gold chandelier above my head. Then they set my hair in curlers, and while it dries, they place my feet in a little claw-foot tub for a warm pre-pedicure foot bath.

Ahhhh.

Even more melty than a hot tub, if you can believe it.

They file and paint my toes gold. Then they do the same to my fingernails.

It's all very glamorous. I feel like Dorothy in *The Wizard of Oz* when she's getting all prettied up before she meets the wizard.

Lana and the queen are both in the royal salon, too.

Lana doesn't say much. Obviously, she can't talk. She doesn't write much, either, though. She just stares into the distance, looking miserable.

On the other hand, the queen doesn't *stop* talking.

'Everyone is coming,' she says. 'Even the royal family of Watermelon will be here. They're bringing their lovely daughter Alison. Lana, darling, she's about your age and goes to school here in Mustard. I hope you two will become friends.'

Lana just shrugs.

A pretty princess named Alison? I can't help but wonder if that's the girl Prince Mortimer marries in the original story. Whatever. She's not marrying him in *this* story.

And: Watermelon? Really?

Once my nails are dry, my hair is arranged in a very cool and elaborate updo, with gold clips to keep it in place. They even sprinkle in gold sparkles to make it shine.

110

Then they get to work on my make-up.

Make-up!

I've used some of my mum's blusher before, just for fun, but I've never had my *make-up* done. They use pink blusher! And gold eye shadow! And mascara! And pink lip gloss! By the time they're done, I look years older. At least thirteen.

Lana is still getting her make-up done, so I tell her I'll meet her in her suite in half an hour to help her get dressed.

One hour until the wedding!

The people around the palace are buzzing and hopping and getting everything ready. I peek into the ballroom to see what it looks like, and there are at least a hundred gold chairs set up with an aisle down the middle.

I practise my wedding walk all the way back to my room. Heel-toe, heel-toe. Slow and steady. I try to keep my shoulders down like my nana always tells me to.

I miss my nana. She would be so proud to know that I'm the Little Mermaid's maid of honour.

I change into my yellow maid-of-honour dress in my room, and then hurry over to Lana's door to see how she's doing. I knock once. Twice. Three times. I can hear her inside, but she's not answering.

Oh, right. She can't talk.

Finally she throws open the door.

She's in her full veil and wedding gown. Her hair hangs loose and curly around her shoulders. She looks gorgeous. Sure, she always looks gorgeous, but now she looks *extra* gorgeous. Like a princess. Like a real princess. No – like a fairy tale princess.

'You look beautiful,' I breathe.

She shrugs.

Then I notice her face.

Her eyes are wide, her skin is pale, and she's biting her lower lip so hard, I think it might be bleeding. She also has her right hand wound through her hair and appears to be pulling on it. Hard. She looks terrified.

'Lana, you don't look so good. I mean, you look gorgeous, but you also kind of look like you're about to puke.'

Just what every bride wants to hear on her wedding day. Maybe I'm not the world's best maid of honour, after all.

Lana closes her eyes and then opens them again, looking even sicker.

I'm not sure what to do. Or what to say. As maid of honour, it's my job to make her feel better. To get her to the altar. But how can I convince her to go through with a wedding when she's so clearly unhappy? On the other hand, if she doesn't marry Prince Mortimer, what will happen to her? Nothing good. Something bad, in fact.

Someone pounds on the door. 'Guys, it's me! Jonah! Can I come in?'

'Yup,' I say, nervously watching Lana.

'Everyone's waiting,' he says, waltzing in. 'Are you two ready?'

Jonah looks adorable. He's in a black tux with a mustard-coloured bow tie. I wish I had a camera to take a picture and show my parents. Although then they would wonder why we were at a fancy event without them. It might be hard to explain.

Lana takes a deep breath. Then she nods. She marches out of the room, and we trail behind her. She'll be happy, right? This will all work out.

It has to work out. Has to, *has* to, HAS to.

And the pit of fear in my stomach has to go away.

We follow Lana down the stairs and towards the ballroom. For some reason, this feels more like a funeral march than a wedding. Maybe that's just how weddings always are? It's not like I've ever been involved in one before. What do I know?

Vivian is waiting for us at the bottom. 'You look beautiful, Princess Lana! You, too, Abby. Take your bouquets.' She hands us both bunches of yellow roses and white baby's-breath, tied together with gold ribbon.

Ohhhh, pretty.

Jonah waves to us and slips inside so he can sit down with the rest of the crowd.

I peek through the open doors and see that the room is packed with at least a hundred people. Prince Mortimer is also in a black tuxedo and a mustard-coloured bow tie, and he's already at the altar. Yellow flowers are everywhere – roses, tulips, daisies, and other kinds that I don't know the names of. The room looks really beautiful. I can't believe they put this all together in three days. It must be a world record.

Violin music begins to play.

'Abby,' Vivian says. 'You're first. Then Lana.'

My turn! I look back at Lana. 'You're okay?'

She nods and motions for me to go.

I don't want to leave her by herself, but I guess that's my job. I take a step. Heel-toe, heel-toe, heel-toe. I'm doing it! I'm doing it! This is fun! I am so acing this. Heel-toe, heel-toe, heel-toe! I did it! I made it the whole way without tripping!

When I get the altar, the prince is smiling at me.

I smile back. Maybe he's not so bad. He loves her, right? He'll make her happy?

He is smiling at me, isn't he? I look behind me and realise he's actually smiling at his reflection in the stained-glass window.

Hmm. Well, at least he's smiling. Smiling's still good, right? He could be frowning at his reflection. That would be worse.

I look up and spot Lana, waiting at the doors.

Everyone stands up and turns to her.

She really does look stunning. She only looks a little bit like she's going to puke, and I'm probably the only one who notices.

The violinist begins to play the 'Here Comes the Bride' march.

Lana doesn't move. She just stares. And stares.

Uh-oh. I motion for her to come.

She stares some more. She pulls her hair. She takes one step forward.

She takes one step back.

And then another step back. Then she spins on her heels and runs the other way.

✳ *Chapter Seventeen* ✳

Better Now Than Later

A rumble goes through the room.

The prince looks at me in surprise. 'Did she just leave?'

'Um...' It definitely seems like she did. 'Maybe she had to pee or something?'

'She couldn't have waited until after the wedding?'

'A girl's gotta go when she's gotta go,' I say, not really believing that:

1. I'm talking to a prince about pee or
2. Lana actually had to pee.

'Why don't I go see what the issue is?' I say nervously. And then, without waiting for a response, I hurry back down the aisle – no time for heel-toe now – and run out of the ballroom.

Should I really check the bathrooms? I realise there's no need to, because as soon as I step out of the ballroom, I see that the front door is wide open.

Lana left the palace. She's officially a runaway bride.

I run right after her and spot her already at the shore, holding up her dress, up to her knees in the water.

'What are you doing?' I ask. 'You're supposed to be getting married!'

She shakes her head.

'You're not getting married?'

She shakes her head again.

'But what about the prince?'

More shaking.

'But you know what this means! If he marries someone else, you'll die!'

Her eyes fill with tears and she nods.

I pace up and down the sand. This is not good. Not good at all. If the prince does marry someone else, she's in serious trouble. We're all in serious trouble, because that's not a happy ending at all. That's a terrible ending. That's the same ending as the original ending! I take a deep breath and try to calm down. It's not like he's going to marry someone else *today*. We have some time to figure this out. Maybe the prince will learn to be less of an idiot and she'll change her mind. Maybe we can find another prince that she would want to marry, and *that* would work instead.

I hear Jonah's voice from the palace door. 'Abby! What's happening?'

I guess I have to tell them the wedding's off. Had I known that cancelling a wedding would be part of my maid-of-honour duties, I might not have been so excited about the job. 'You stay here,' I say finally. 'Don't go in the water. I don't want you drowning. I'm going to talk to Prince Mortimer.'

She closes her eyes in relief and I slowly make my way back to the palace.

Everyone looks up at me as I enter the ballroom.

'She had better be coming now,' Prince Mortimer barks. His face is bright red. He looks furious.

'Um, I don't think she is,' I say timidly from about halfway down the aisle.

'Darling, how long will she be?' the queen asks, checking her gold wristwatch.

'A pretty long time,' I say. 'I think she wants to…' I have to just say it. 'I think she wants to cancel the wedding.'

Several hundred gasps echo through the room. I wince.

'You're kidding!'

'Cancel the wedding?'

'Not marry the prince?'

'Is she *crazy*?'

Prince Mortimer's face falls. 'I can't believe she would do that to me,' he cries, looking genuinely pained.

As insensitive as he's been, I can't help but feel bad for him. No one wants to be left at the altar.

The queen jumps up. 'How dare she run off like that?'

The king stands up beside her and turns to the crowd. 'Dudes, we know you all came to see a royal a wedding today, and we *will* have a royal wedding today. Morty, there must be someone else here that you could marry.'

My heart stops. What? Is he kidding? He must be kidding.

The queen nods. 'Yes! Princess Alison is here today. Morty, would you marry her?'

'Let me see her,' Prince Mortimer says.

The queen motions to Princess Alison. 'Sweetie, will you stand up, please?'

Princess Alison stands up and curtsies. She has tight spiral curls and looks familiar. I know! She's the girl from the school, the one who got help after we found Prince Mortimer on Crescent Beach! She's the princess of Watermelon? Not surprisingly, she's wearing a satiny red dress, with a green sash and green shoes.

The prince nods. 'I'll marry her. I like her hair. She's pretty.'

The king claps. 'Fantastic. Alison, would you like to marry our son?'

'Yeah, okay,' she says, twisting a curl around her finger and snapping her chewing gum. 'He is good-looking.'

'And your parents? The king and queen of the kingdom of Watermelon? Do you agree to this union?'

'We do!' the king says, a big, smug smile on his face, a red-and-green checkered bow tie around his neck.

This isn't happening. THIS ISN'T HAPPENING.

'This isn't happening!' I yell.

Jonah tugs on my arm and whispers, 'I'm pretty sure it *is* happening.'

'Great,' Prince Mortimer says. 'Let's start the music again. Do you want to do the whole walk-down-the-aisle thing, or just come up?'

'I'll just come up,' Princess Alison says. She manoeuvres her way through the crowd, fluffs her dress and begins walking down the remainder of the aisle. 'Excuse me,' she says to Jonah and me as she squeezes past us.

'What a perfect match,' a woman sitting near us says.

'She's a princess, he's a prince. He's handsome and she's beautiful. They go together like chips and mustard!'

'What is wrong with you people?' I shriek. 'Mustard does not go on chips! Ketchup goes on chips! Ketchup! Or mayonnaise, in some countries. Or maybe a mixture of the two, if you're into that. But not mustard! Never mustard!'

Everyone stares at me.

Am I losing it?

'I totally agree,' Jonah says. 'C'mon, Abby, let's go. We need to help Lana.'

Yes, we definitely need to help her. Because Prince Mortimer is marrying someone else, which means that Lana is going to DIE in the morning.

Unless we can save her.

* Chapter Eighteen *

Night Swimming

We find Lana sitting on the sand, staring sadly into the sunset.

'You need to go and talk to the sea witch,' I tell her. Lana has to convince the witch to reverse the spell.

She points to her mouth and then her chest.

'You can't breathe underwater,' I say.

She nods.

'Any way we can get the sea witch to come ashore?' I ask.

Lana shakes her head and shimmies her hand so it looks like a tail.

'She doesn't have legs,' I confirm. 'But she's a witch; she can do whatever she wants.'

'She probably doesn't want to come on land,' Jonah says. He can be annoyingly logical.

Argh! We have to fix this! We're running out of time!

'Maybe Princess Alison won't *really* marry Prince Mortimer,' Jonah says. 'Maybe she'll pull a Lana, and bolt at the last minute.'

Just then we hear loud clapping inside the palace and choruses of 'Congratulations!'

'There goes that idea,' I mumble.

'Oh! Oh!' Jonah shrieks. 'What about that potion Carolyn talked about? Remember? The one that her great-great-grandmother used to go underwater? The spit potion?'

I shake my head. 'Do you think that even works?'

'Well, she should try it. What other choice do we have?'

He has a point.

We find Carolyn in the kitchen, slicing lemons.

'Remember that potion you said your great-great-grandmother used to go underwater?' I ask.

'How could I forget?' she says with a laugh.

'Do you know how to make it?'

'Do I remember the ingredients? Of course I do;

mermaid's spit, a tablespoon of sea salt, three fish eggs, a tablespoon of water, a teaspoon of sparkling water, and a pinch of algae. I've always wanted to make it, but finding the mermaid's spit has been difficult.'

'We have the spit,' I say. 'We need some potion so Lana can go underwater.'

'Of course,' she says, putting down her knife. 'Anything for my favourite mermaid.'

She gathers all the stuff from the kitchen, mixes it up in a glass, and then runs with us outside and hands the glass to Lana. Lana spits inside, then takes a sip. Then she turns and hurries into the ocean, diving underwater. Two seconds later she pops up, gasping and shaking her head.

'I guess it doesn't work,' I say.

'Maybe now that Lana has legs, her spit isn't mermaid-y any more,' Carolyn says.

Lana leans over and carves into the sand: 'I DON'T HAVE A TAIL BUT I WILL ALWAYS BE A MERMAID.'

'In that case,' Jonah says, 'maybe a mermaid can't use her own spit. Or maybe the spell only works on humans.'

'Lana's a human,' I say.

Carolyn shakes her head. 'She's a mermaid. She just said so herself.'

Jonah tugs on my hand. 'You know what that means, right? It might work on us.'

Huh? 'Us?'

'Us,' he repeats. 'We're human.'

'I am, yes. I'm not always so sure about you.'

'Seriously, Abby. *We'll* try the potion.'

'I doubt it will work,' I say, my heart hammering.

'I bet it will,' he says. 'We'll get to breathe underwater! It'll be fun!'

'Sharks. Waves. Salt in our mouths. That doesn't sound like fun. And it's going to be dark soon. How will we see anything?' I can't do it. I just can't.

'Don't you have a light on your watch?' he asks.

'Yeah.' As if one probably-waterproof-watch light is enough for me to go up against the entire ocean.

'Let's just try. It's our only chance.'

'Are there any other options?' I ask, my voice squeaky. 'There must be. Maybe Carolyn wants to try it?'

Carolyn shakes her head. 'Me? Are you crazy? I eat shark. I don't let them eat me!'

'You eat shark?' Jonah asks, eyes wide.

She nods. 'I'll make it for you. It's delicious.'

'No thanks,' we say in unison.

Jonah looks at me. 'I think it's up to us, then. Let's do it!'

Goose bumps cover my whole body. He wants me to go underwater. No life jacket. No air.

I can't. I can't. I can't.

I *have* to.

Slowly I nod.

Lana hands Jonah the cup.

'Cheers!' Jonah cries, and takes a big sip. 'It tastes like sushi!'

I roll my eyes. 'Have you ever even had sushi?'

'No, but I bet this is what it tastes like. It could use some ketchup.' When Jonah's finished, he hands me the cup and scurries towards the water, diving right in.

'Wait, Jonah!' I yell, but it's too late. He's under.

He pops up. 'It works! It really works!'

'Great. Just, um, great!' My hands shake. Before I sip, I ask, 'But how will we ever find the sea witch?'

'Lana can make us a map,' Jonah calls.

Carolyn takes a pen and paper out of her apron and hands it to Lana. 'Here you go.'

Lana starts to sketch. When she's finished, she writes '2 HOURS' on top.

'It'll take us two hours to get there?' I ask.

Lana nods.

That's a long time for us to be swimming. Two hours to the sea witch's place, two hours back, plus how long to convince the witch to help us? At least we have twelve hours to work with.

'Bottoms up,' Carolyn says.

I nod, and then I swallow a gulp of the potion. I almost gag. But I keep swallowing because I have to.

P.S. My brother's not wrong – a little ketchup *would* go a long way.

I hand Lana the glass and then carefully wade into the water. The *dark* water. This can't be a good idea. I barely swim well during the day; how am I going to swim well at night?

'Just dunk!' Jonah orders me.

I bristle at being bossed around by my baby brother, but I know he's right. Getting into the water is like taking off a plaster. It always hurts less to just rip it off. I'm in up to my waist. I should go under now.

Okay, *now*.

'Time is ticking,' Jonah calls. 'I'm going under again!'

'Jonah, hold on!' I yell, but then he disappears under the surf. At first I see bubbles rise to the surface but then they stop.

I don't like bubbles that stop. My heart feels like it might pound out of my chest.

Now I have no choice. I grip the map in my hand, hold my nose with the other, seal my eyes shut, and go under.

Cold, cold, cold! I carefully open my left eye. At first it's blurry, but then it clears up. This is a hopeful sign. It doesn't sting or anything. I open the right eye.

Around me I see blue. Lots and lots of navy blue. I'm glad the sun isn't completely gone yet.

'Hi!' Jonah says, swimming over to me. 'How cool is this? We can talk!'

I am afraid to open my mouth in case I swallow a gallon of water and drown. But I do it. I open my lips in a little circle and take a tiny breath in. I do not choke.

'It works!' I say, amazed. I have no idea *how* it works, but it is working. I am breathing and talking underwater. No scuba equipment necessary.

I thought I would sink to the bottom, but I'm not. I'm just floating. It's like I'm in one of those gravity-less spaceships and I can go up or down or anywhere I want.

We swim further into the deep.

There are brightly coloured fish swimming in all directions. A family of turtles meanders by us. And coral is everywhere. It looks like pipe cleaners gently blowing in the wind. Yellow, red, orange, blue, green. The water doesn't even feel cold any more, just like a really nice bath.

Jonah is having the time of his life. He's laughing, somersaulting. He's even yodeling. Does he really have to let every sea creature know we're here?

'Can you try to be quiet?' I ask him, as a neon fish that's shaped like a trumpet smashes its nose against my knee. It does not seem to like me.

'Why? This is awesome.'

'Jonah! This is serious business! You've been acting like a two-year-old since we got here!'

'You've been acting like a forty-year-old!' he snaps back. 'This is supposed to be fun.'

'No, it isn't!' I yell back as the trumpet fish goes after my big toe. 'We're helping Lana.'

'Why can't helping Lana be fun?'

'Because...because... You're impossible,' I say, and turn my back on him. 'Let's go to the sea witch and get this over with.' We have to stay on schedule. We have to see the sea witch. But first we have to *find* the sea witch.

I pull the map up to my eyes. Unfortunately, the map has disintegrated in the water.

'Crumbs!' I yell.

Jonah turns back to me. 'What's wrong?'

'Unlike us, the map was not waterproof.'

He bites his lower lip. 'I think I remember the way. Follow me.'

'You think, or you *know*?'

He shrugs. 'I think.'

'Time is ticking, Jonah!'

'Well,' he says, swimming forward, 'then we'd better get kicking.'

I nervously follow Jonah through seaweed, around coral, and over a cave. I feel bad for snapping at him, but honestly, he doesn't take anything seriously.

By now the water has started to get dark. Really dark. I press the light on my watch to illuminate our path and pray that the batteries don't die.

We swim for what feels like at least another hour.

I could really do with a snack. That sushi potion was just not enough. I wish I'd had time to pack a picnic lunch from the wedding buffet. I'm going to miss that lemon meringue pie.

At the end of the cave, Jonah turns left and points.

'That's it,' he says.

I shine my light up ahead. I have no doubt that he's right. If someone asked me to design a sea witch's house, this is what I'd create.

The walls are grey stone and covered in black sea-sludge. The path to the doorway is surrounded by barracudas and floating fish skeletons. There's a low moaning sound all around us. Jonah slows down and takes my hand.

'Maybe we should find a doorbell or something. The sea witch might not be the type of person who likes to be surprised.' I see a big knocker in the shape of a human skull. With a trembling hand, I bang the knocker against the door.

Slowly the door creeps open.

'Come in,' we hear. The voice is definitely female, but low and raspy.

We swim through the entranceway, terrified.

There she sits in the middle of the room. Well, not sits. Lies sideways on a black couch. She is not what I expected at all. She's beautiful. She's a mermaid just like Lana, but her tail is dark purple instead of green and orange. She's younger than I expected, too – she looks about my mum's age. She has black, waist-length hair.

Beside the couch is a large grey pot. No, it's not a pot. It's a cauldron. It's made of stone, and bubbles are steaming out of it. It looks like a hot tub – but a really, really scary one. I do not want to go anywhere near that cauldron if I can help it. I take a step back.

'Who are you?' the sea witch drawls. Her voice is smoky. It makes me want to move closer, but I resist.

'I'm-I'm-I'm Abby,' I stutter. 'And this is my brother, Jonah.'

'Hello,' she says. 'I'm Nelly.'

I nod. 'We're here on behalf of Lana. I'm her—' I pause. 'I'm her lawyer.'

The sea witch cackles. 'Her lawyer? Lana has a lawyer?'

I nod. 'And I'm here to negotiate a deal.'

'How are you even down here? Did you take the underwater potion?'

We nod.

Nelly laughs again. 'Well, you'd better start negotiating before your time runs out.'

'Right.' I nervously clear my throat. It's been about two hours, which means we have ten hours left. We can convince her to help us in ten hours, can't we? 'We would like you to reverse the spell you put on Lana,' I say, my voice trembling.

She raises a perfectly arched eyebrow. 'Which one?'

I half smile. 'All of them?'

'Let's see,' Nelly says. 'There's the spell that changed her tail into legs. There's the spell that took away her voice. Then there's the spell that says that if the prince marries anyone else, she'll die before the next sunrise, which is at six oh five A.M.'

'All of them would be good,' I say. 'But the dying one is definitely our priority.'

'Reversing spells isn't cheap. What will you give me?'

I clear my throat. 'What do you want?' Oops. This may have been a tiny oversight on my part. I came to negotiate with the sea witch but I didn't bring anything to trade. Never mind being a failed maid of honour – I'm a failed lawyer, too.

Nelly eyes Jonah. 'The boy?'

Jonah scoots into my side.

'Um, no.' Even though we're kind of in a fight, she still can't have my brother. 'Is there anything else you want?'

She looks me over. 'What is that on your wrist?'

I look down. 'You want my watch? I can give you my watch.' Not that I really want to give away my watch, but of course I'll do it to save Lana's *life*. I'm not sure how we'll find our way back to the shore without any light, though. I guess I'll worry about that problem later.

The sea witch nods. 'Here's my offer. You give me the watch.'

'Okay,' I say. Maybe this won't be so hard after all.

'And in return for the watch, I'll give you a knife. You'll use the knife to stab the prince in the heart. Then I'll undo all the spells. Lana can go back to her life as a mermaid.'

Is she kidding me?

'Um, that's not going to work, either,' I say. 'I am not going to kill someone.' Sure, the prince is a bit of an idiot, but that doesn't mean I want him dead. And that definitely doesn't mean that I would ever consider killing him. I want to *be* a lawyer, not *need* a lawyer. 'Can't I just give you the watch, and you'll reverse the spells?'

She snorts. 'Reverse all the spells for one measly watch? No. One of you stabs the prince, or nothing. You know what? I don't even want a watch. The girl and I had a deal. She's the one who wasn't satisfied with her life even though she had *everything*. She had family who loved her! She was a princess! She was beautiful! But no, no, no, she wanted to give it all up to be *human*. She's an idiot! Just like her father!'

'But she wasn't happy!' I say. 'She risked everything for a different life. She's not an idiot. She's...she's...brave! And you're a coward. You just hide in your cave and steal from people. You want everyone to be as miserable as you are.'

Nelly blinks. And then blinks again. 'Unless you have something better than a watch to trade, then we're finished here.'

Now what are we supposed to do? Wait. 'Why is Lana's dad an idiot?' I wonder aloud.

She ignores my question and instead says, 'I guess we're finished. Samuel! My dear Samuel! Show these children the door!'

My dear Samuel? 'Don't tell me she has a boyfriend,' I say.

134

But no. Just then a shark – an actual shark – swims up to us with a menacing look on its face.

I'm not that surprised her only companion is a shark – no person could love someone that mean.

'We're getting out of here,' I say, and pull Jonah straight out of the house.

By the time we reach the black water, my heart is beating about three thousand miles a minute.

'That didn't go well,' Jonah says.

'No, it didn't,' I say, leaning against something soft and squishy that I hope won't eat me. I try to catch my breath. 'Now what?'

'I can think of one person who might help us,' Jonah says.

'Who?'

'The Sea King.'

I nod. 'It's time to find Lana's dad.'

✳ *Chapter Nineteen* ✳

Sticks and Stones

'I remember that, in the film, the king offers to swap places with the Little Mermaid,' Jonah explains as we start swimming again. 'Maybe he'll want to do that now.'

My heart clenches. 'So the king dies instead of Lana? We don't want that, either!'

'Hopefully he'll have a better idea than that,' Jonah says. 'But we have to find him and ask. Don't you think our parents would want to know if we were facing a life-or-death situation?'

'We face life-and-death situations every time we go into the mirror!' I say.

'True,' Jonah says. 'But still.'

'Okay,' I say. Maybe the king can force the witch to

recant her spell. Or maybe he'll have something to trade. Clearly he knows the sea witch – she called him an idiot.

So we're going to talk to him. But first we have to find him. Which we can't seem to do. We swim and swim, but we keep passing the same cave.

We're lost. We're very, very lost.

And there's something really freaky about being lost underwater in the dark. Beige coral sways in the wind and looks like fingers trying to grab us. Silvery fish appear to have teeth.

I light up my watch. It says six thirty, which means it must be around midnight here. How much longer can we swim in circles?

'We know you,' a voice says.

'Did you say something?' Jonah asks.

'No,' I say. 'I thought it was you.' A chill creeps down my spine. 'Hello?' I say timidly. 'Is someone there?'

'Yes,' another voice says.

'We are,' says a third voice.

We're surrounded.

'Who are you?' I ask, and aim my watch light at the voices. The light reveals a mermaid. No – five mermaids. All with green-and-orange swishing tails. The tops they're wearing look familiar, but I can't figure out from where.

'We're Lana's sisters,' the one in the middle says. She

has short, butter-coloured hair and she's wearing a white jumper. 'We've been spying on her, but we can't get too close to the shore. Is Lana okay?'

'Not exactly,' I say, before explaining the whole story.

'We have to go amd talk to my dad!' one sister wearing a purple hoodie cries. 'He has to help.'

'We were trying to find him,' I say. 'Isn't it the middle of the night? What were you guys doing?'

'We were at a party,' another one says, giving the necklace she's wearing an anxious twirl. Her brown hair is tied back in a tight braid and she's wearing a light-green T-shirt with a collar. 'It's past curfew, though – we're definitely going to get in trouble.'

'It's worth it for Lana,' the mermaid in the hoodie says. 'Follow me!'

We follow her through a winding path, past schools of striped and speckled fish, sparkly red coral, and even a twenty-foot-long shipwreck that's jammed into some rocks.

Two of the sisters swim by me, both wearing what look a lot like pyjama tops.

Familiar pyjama tops.

I glance at all the sisters. Purple hoodie. Green T-shirt. White jumper. Wait a sec.

'Those are my clothes!' I exclaim. 'You found my suitcase!'

They spin around. 'That was yours?' the one in the hoodie asks.

'Yes!' I say. 'I thought I lost it.'

'You did lose it,' the one with the braid mutters. 'Finders keepers.' She looks like the youngest of the lot.

'Sasha,' the one with the short hair and white jumper scolds. 'We'll give them back their stuff.' She looks like the oldest.

'Can we keep the wood paddles and the ball?' the one in my hoodie asks. 'We made up a whole game with them where we hit the ball back and forth.'

'That's how you're supposed to play,' Jonah says. 'It's called Kadima.'

'We love Kadima,' she says.

'Me too!' Jonah says. 'We should play if we have time.'

'There's no time for Kadima!' the oldest sister and I both yell. We look at each other and smile.

Soon we get to what appears to be a town. It's pretty empty because it's the middle of the night, but there's one restaurant still open.

'Where are we?' I ask.

'That's Salties,' one of the sisters tells me. 'It's the

139

nicest restaurant on the Main Canal.'

A few mermaids and mermen are sitting outside, enjoying the night. Instead of being pitch-black, like I expected, there are little sparkling lights lining the canal.

'Where do the lights come from?' I ask the oldest sister.

'Bioluminescence,' she says. 'Underwater life that glows in the dark.'

Everyone looks at us curiously as we swim past – we are the only ones without tails – but we don't stop to sightsee.

Finally we spot what has to be the castle.

It's just as nice, if not nicer, than Prince Mortimer's palace. It's made of stone and cliffs and covered in protective coral.

'Let's go straight to Dad's room,' the oldest says. 'Follow me!'

No need for stairs in this palace. We swim right up into the king's windowless room. Not much security here.

'Dad! Dad!' the oldest one cries, swimming over to his bed.

'What's wrong, girls?' the king asks, opening his eyes.

He has dark hair that's grey at the temples. He also has one of those chins with a cleft in it.

He spots us. 'Why did you bring humans?'

140

'They're friends of Lana's. And Lana needs our help.'

Quickly I spill out the whole story. '...So you see,' I say once I've finished, 'we didn't know who else to go to. Do you have anything the sea witch would want? Or could you command her to reverse the spell? Maybe threaten to put her in ocean prison?'

The king looks shocked, yet I notice a determined glint in his eye. 'Poor Lana! We must save her at once. Girls! Collect all the family jewels. The necklaces! The rings! All of Mum's old stuff!'

'Not the jewellery!' one of the sisters cries. 'It's all we have left of Mum!'

'Your mum would want us to use it.' The king throws off his covers. 'Everyone, follow me.'

✳ *Chapter Twenty* ✳

We're Back

'It's not the most inviting décor,' I say as I push a floating fish skeleton out of the way and knock on the door. I glance at my watch. We have to move fast. We've been underwater for almost nine-and-a-half hours. We still need two hours to get back to the beach.

'Go away!' Nelly yells from inside. 'Didn't I tell you to stop bothering me?'

The door swings open and the sea witch has a scowl on her face. But suddenly her expression changes. Softens. She blinks. And then blinks again. She's looking above my head and I turn to see that she's staring at the king.

And he's staring at her.

'What do *you* want?' she asks.

The king blushes.

'Nelly,' I say, 'the king is here to offer you jewellery. If you'll save his daughter.'

'Right!' the king says, snapping out of his trance. 'May we come in?'

Nelly tears her eyes away from the king and checks out our whole group. 'All of you?'

'Yes,' I say. I put my hands on my hips and clench them into fists, hoping I look defiant.

'I guess.' Nelly sweeps her arm to the side in an exaggerated gesture of welcome, and all eight of us float-march in.

'I haven't seen you in years,' the king says.

'No, you haven't,' Nelly says, tight-lipped.

'How do you know each other?' I ask.

'We went to primary school together,' the king says.

'We certainly did,' Nelly says, crossing her arms and slapping her tail against the ground. 'How could I forget? You used to call me a horrible name.'

The king's eyes widen in surprise. 'What are you talking about? I called you Jelly Nelly!'

She scowls. 'Exactly. Jelly Nelly. Because I reminded you of a jellyfish.'

'So why is that horrible?' the king asks, his forehead wrinkling.

'Because jellyfish are annoying and poisonous,' Nelly spits out.

I'd have to agree. Jellyfish are kind of the mosquitoes of the sea.

The king shakes his head. 'Jellyfish are clever. And beautiful. And fascinating.'

'They are not,' Nelly says, but her voice wavers.

'They are so,' he says. 'I called you Jelly Nelly because I had a crush on you.'

Nelly blushes. 'You did?'

'You did?' we all echo.

Now it's the king's turn to blush.

Nelly makes a strange sound. Was it a giggle? She clears her throat. 'Oh. I just assumed...' Her voice trails off. 'I had no idea.' She wraps a strand of her dark hair around her finger. She giggles again. Is Nelly flirting? Does the sea witch *like* the king?

'Well, now you know,' he says. He's all flushed. 'It's nice to see you again.' Oh. My. Goodness. Does he still *like* the witch?

But then he shakes his head. 'No. It's *not* nice. You have to help my daughter.'

Nelly crosses her arms. 'I don't have to do anything.'

He straightens up, flirting forgotten. 'We have jewels to offer you. In exchange for you changing the spell you

144

put on Lana. Girls, show her what you have. Nelly, take whatever you want. But please, spare my daughter.'

The oldest steps up and opens her hand to reveal a sparkling ring. 'I have a diamond engagement ring.'

The second oldest opens her hand next. 'I have emerald earrings.'

The third shows us a chunky bracelet. 'It's fourteen-carat gold.'

The fourth has two hoop earrings dangling on her thumb. 'They're platinum.'

Sasha, the youngest, steps up and points to her neck. 'I'm wearing a mother-of-pearl necklace. I guess you can have it.'

Hold on a minute. 'That's my necklace!' I exclaim.

Sasha shrugs. 'Don't you want to help Lana?'

I sigh. 'You can have it,' I tell Nelly.

Nelly eyes the goods. 'Hmm,' she says. 'They're pretty, but I already have my own jewellery.' She wiggles her fingers in front of us, and we see that they are glittering with jewels. 'Do you have anything else?'

'Um…' We look at each other. We are empty-handed. We are out of stuff.

'You can have my Kadima paddles,' Jonah offers.

'What's Kadima?' Nelly asks, intrigued.

'It's a game,' Jonah says. 'You and another person hit

a ball back and forth. It's lots of fun.'

Nelly's face clouds over. 'I don't want a game,' she snarls. 'Who am I going to play it with? Samuel doesn't have hands. If you have nothing else to offer, I think we're finished here.'

A lightbulb goes off in my head. She doesn't want Kadima *paddles*. She wants someone to play Kadima *with*.

Before I thought no one could love her because she was mean. But maybe she's so mean because no one loves her.

I know how to save Lana.

'Would you consider reversing the spells on Lana in exchange for a date?' I blurt out.

Nelly blinks. 'Excuse me?'

'A date,' I repeat. My mouth feels dry. This has to work. It just has to.

Nelly blushes and looks down at the sandy floor. 'A date with whom?'

I glance at the king. His cheeks are just as red as Nelly's. He's just as lonely as Nelly.

He swims forward. 'With me,' he says.

Their eyes meet across the room.

'Really?' she asks softly.

He nods. He takes another step toward her. 'Would you like to go out sometime, Jelly Nelly? Or I can just

146

call you Nelly.'

'Just Nelly is good,' she says. And then giggles.

Yes! This is going to work! Way to go, me! Speaking of going – we have to get a move on.

'So do we have a deal?' I ask. 'A date in exchange for reversing the spells? You can go to Salties!'

'What if she hurts our dad?' the youngest mermaid cries. 'She's a witch, and he's all we have left!'

Good point.

'Can you give us some sort of collateral?' the oldest mermaid asks, running her fingers through her short hair.

Nelly nods toward the shark. 'You can keep Samuel as a pet until the date is over. He needs a babysitter, anyway. He eats the couch when he's lonely.'

Better the couch than me.

'So,' I ask again. 'Do we have a deal?'

We all hold our breath.

Nelly and the king nod. 'Deal,' they say simultaneously, and then they both laugh and turn red again.

'Let's shake on it,' the king says, putting out his hand.

'Abby,' Jonah says, tugging at my sleeve.

'One sec, Jonah,' I say, wanting to see how this ends.

Nelly takes his outstretched hand.

We wait for them to shake, but instead, they both just stand there, holding each other's hands. And holding.

147

Still holding.

All righty, then.

'Abby,' Jonah says again. 'I don't feel so good. My chest feels heavy.'

I glance at my watch. The potion is going to run out in two hours! We have to go.

'Abby,' Jonah says again, and crumples into a heap on the sandy ground.

I lunge after him. But before I can reach him, the room starts to spin. I feel intense pressure on my chest. Like someone's sitting on me. Or like I'm underwater and I can't breathe.

Oh, no.

The potion ran out early.

'Jonah!' I try to yell – but nothing comes out. The people around me look murkier and murkier until I can't see anything at all.

✳ *Chapter Twenty-one* ✳

Ashore

'Abby, Abby. You have to get up.'

The next thing I see is light. A very bright light.

I open my eyes. Where am I? What happened?

I sit up, cough and notice Lana kneeling beside me.

'Finally,' she says, her eyes squinting in concern. 'How do you feel?'

The last thing I remember, Jonah and I were underwater. And now it's just me and Lana on the beach. I'm so confused. 'How did I get here?'

'My family brought you up, and then I pulled you onto the beach.'

I'm still a bit dizzy and disoriented.

Wait a sec. I'm on the beach. Jonah's not. Oh, no. Oh no, oh no, oh no. 'Where's my brother?'

She hesitates. 'He's, um…'

My heart stops. He drowned. He drowned, and it's all my fault. Plus I was so mean to him today. I was awful. He was just being his totally awesome fun self, and I yelled at him. I try to breathe, but I can't.

'…There he is,' she says.

What? He's alive? I jump to my feet and spot him hopping his way down the beach.

'Jonah!' I shriek. 'You're alive!' I throw my arms around his neck.

'Of course I'm alive,' he says. 'I was just getting myself a snack. I'm starving.' He's munching on chips and mustard. 'Glad you're finally awake.'

I let go of his neck even though I don't want to. 'How long was I out for?'

'A few hours.'

'What happened?'

'Either we didn't take enough potion each, or the recipe wasn't exactly right.'

I hug him hard. 'I'm so sorry I was mean to you.'

'I'm sorry I made you do all the work,' he says. 'Want a chip? The mustard isn't as awful as you'd think.'

'Sure,' I say.

'Me too,' Lana says.

'What time is it?' I wonder.

'Almost ten A.M.'

I look at Lana in surprise. 'It's ten o'clock, and you're still alive!'

She nods. 'I am.'

'And you can talk!'

She nods again. 'Nelly reversed the spell. And gave me back my voice.'

'That's amazing!' I cheer. 'We did it! We fixed the story! Everything is back the way it was!'

'Not everything,' Jonah says.

'What do you mean?' I ask, munching on another chip. Jonah's right. The mustard isn't that bad.

He motions to Lana. 'She still has legs.'

He's right. She *does* still have legs. 'What happened? Nelly wouldn't let you have your tail back? She's making you stay on land forever? I thought we had done so well! Did your dad cancel the date or something?'

Lana shakes her head. 'No, that's not it. She offered to give me my tail back, but I told her I didn't want it.'

Huh? 'Why not?'

'I love my family, but I don't want to leave the surface. Prince or not, it's my home now. I love to walk and dance.

151

And I really love sunsets. And shoops – I mean, shoes. And books. And paintings. And have you tried a cheeseburger with mustard and that yellow-y American cheese? They're amazing.'

I nod.

She goes on. 'And even though I have my voice back, I have another voice now that I'm not ready to give up.'

I don't understand what she's talking about. 'You have a second voice?'

'Yes! Thanks to you, I can write! And that's given me a whole new voice. I want to stay on land and write stories about the world under the ocean. I want to write books about mermaids and share them with humans so they don't think merfolk are make-believe!'

'I would love to read those,' I say. 'Is your dad okay with you staying?'

She nods. 'He said he was going to miss me, but he also gave me these.' She opens her hand, and I see the diamond ring, the emerald earrings, and the bracelet. 'They belonged to my mother. He told me I can sell them and buy a house with a big dock so he and my sisters can always visit.'

'That's amazing,' I say, throwing my arms around Lana in a hug. 'Everything worked out.'

'Almost,' Jonah says. 'We still have to get home.'

Oh, no! If it's almost ten here, we only have two hours to get back, and we still have no idea how. 'What are we going to do?' I ask.

'It's all taken care of,' Jonah says smugly. 'By me.'

'But, Jonah, we're sitting on the beach. Not in our basement.'

'Not for long,' Jonah says, and then he points to the water.

In the distance, I see the five mermaid sisters, plus Nelly, plus the king.

'She's finally awake!' the oldest mermaid says.

'Hi, guys!' Lana yells. She splashes out into the water and hugs them all. Aw. We got them back together.

'Carolyn made us more underwater potion,' Jonah says. 'She made double, just to be safe.'

'How does that help?' I ask. 'We don't live underwater.'

'Nelly's cauldron is underwater. It's going to take us home.'

'But Nelly isn't a fairy,' I say. 'Is she?'

He shrugs. 'She said she could do it.'

'She did? Did you have to give her something?'

He shook his head. 'She said it's payment for reintroducing her to the king.'

'Oh!' If being a judge doesn't work out, maybe I can be a matchmaker. 'When do we go?'

'Now!'

I look back up at the palace. 'Should we say goodbye?'

'I said goodbye for both of us. Carolyn said she'll miss us. And she promised to teach Lana how to cook.'

'Don't worry,' Lana says. '*I* promise not to make shark.'

'And Vivian packed up all our things and put them in the suitcase.'

'Whose suitcase?'

'Your suitcase! The mermaids gave it back.'

'Oh! Great! What about the stuff inside the suitcase?'

'They gave that back, too. Lana put your necklace around your neck when you were sleeping. I tried to do it myself, but that clasp is really confusing.'

I reach up and feel my necklace. 'Thanks, Jonah. Thanks, Lana.'

'No problem,' Lana says.

'I gave Lana's sisters my Kadima paddles,' Jonah says. 'They seemed to really like them.'

'That was sweet of you, Jonah.' I turn to Lana.

Lana takes the cup of potion, spits in it, and then hands it to me. 'I'm going to miss you two. Thank you for everything.'

I chug the still-disgusting potion, and then give Lana a tight hug. 'Your stories are going to be amazing.'

'Thanks. I can't wait to write them.'

Jonah gives her a hug, too.

'I'll see you tomorrow, everyone!' she calls to her family. 'Have fun on your date, Dad! But don't make any trades, okay? And I really will miss you, Abby and Jonah!'

We wave. Here we go. With one hand, I hold on to my brother, and with the other, I hold on to my suitcase. Just like when I came, but now with extra yellow clothes. I dunk right away.

Sometimes you just have to go for it.

This time when we go underwater, the ocean is alive with activity. Mermaids and mermen everywhere. Everyone's busy, swimming this way or that. It's like we were dropped in the busiest aquarium in the world.

I wish we had more time to explore. Maybe we'll come back one day.

When we arrive at Nelly's house, everything looks different. Maybe because it's bright outside. Or maybe because she did some spring cleaning of the skeletons and stuff.

'Thank you,' Nelly whispers to me.

I try not to stiffen as she gives me a hug.

'Because we reintroduced you to the king?' I ask.

'Yes. And because you were right. Instead of changing my own life, I wanted everyone to be as miserable as I was. I *was* a coward.'

We hug all the sisters, and then we are ready to go. 'What do we do?' I ask, eyeing the bubbling cauldron with a little bit of fear.

'Just swim right into it,' Nelly says.

'We won't get burnt?'

'You shouldn't.'

'But I don't understand,' I say. 'I thought only fairies could get us home.'

'I *am* a fairy,' she says.

Huh? 'We thought you were a witch,' Jonah says.

'A witch is a fairy who does bad things,' she says. 'See, it depends what you use your magic for.'

Aha. That makes sense. I look towards the cauldron. 'We can't both fit in,' I say. Not together.

'I'll go first,' Jonah says.

'I'm not letting you go alone!' I say.

'Then hold on to my foot.'

'Okay,' I say. I grab hold of his very wet trainer with one hand and the suitcase with the other. 'Ready?' I ask.

'Ready!' he says. 'Hold on tight!'

He swims, swims, swims us right towards the cauldron. It squeezes but doesn't hurt. I close my eyes and trust Jonah to get us home.

✳ *Chapter Twenty-two* ✳

Dry, Again

The next thing I know, I'm in a very large puddle on my basement floor, still holding Jonah's foot. We've slid across half the floor like we're at a water park.

'Well done,' I hear.

'You too,' Jonah and I both say at the same time.

'That wasn't me,' I say. My spine tingles. 'That wasn't you?'

He shakes his head.

'But, Jonah, if it wasn't me, and it wasn't you...' I look back at the mirror. It's still swirling. 'Maryrose? Was that you?'

She doesn't answer. But that had to have been her! It

must have been! She talked to us! She finally talked to us! And she said, 'Well done'!

What does 'well done' mean? 'Was changing the tale what we were supposed to do?' I ask the mirror. 'Do you have a plan for us?'

She still doesn't answer.

'Abby, what time is it?' Jonah asks.

I look at my watch. 'It's four minutes to seven.'

'We've got to go!'

He's right. Our parents will be going to wake us up any minute. I turn back to the mirror. 'I have a lot of questions for you,' I say. 'And next time, I would really appreciate it if you could answer them.' I leave the wet suitcase downstairs because it's filled with water and ridiculously heavy. I cross my fingers and hope I have a chance to deal with it before my parents find it.

We dash up the stairs. When we're on the main floor, I hear the ringing of my parents' alarm clock. 'Run! Run!' I whisper to Jonah. 'Go and put on your pjs, hide your wet clothes in the back of your wardrobe, and get into bed! Love you! I'm glad you didn't drown!'

'Love you, too!' Jonah says as he sprints towards his bedroom. 'I'm glad you didn't drown, either!'

Our doors close just as I hear my parents' door opening. Oh no, oh no, oh no! I rip off my clothes, look for a clean pair of pyjamas, remember I don't have any, jump under my covers, and pull them up to my neck as my doorknob starts to wiggle.

About half a second later, my door creeps open. 'Morning, honey,' my mum says. 'Time to get up.'

I fake a yawn. 'Thanks, Mum!'

I hear a bang from Jonah's room. Mum looks quizzically in his direction. Oh, no! He's not ready yet. I need to distract her! What do I do?

'Wait! Mum?'

She leans against the doorway. 'Yes, honey?'

'I want to talk to you about something.'

'Yes?' she asks expectantly.

At first I have no idea what I want to say, but then, suddenly, I do.

I spot my jewellery box on my dresser and think about Lana. I had wanted her to accept her life as it was, but she wanted to fight for her dreams. Sure, sometimes you have to get what you get and not get upset. But maybe other times, you have to follow your heart and go after what you really want. Take a risk. Be brave.

I guess part of growing up is learning when to do which.

'Mum,' I start. 'I know you're really busy. I understand. But I think I'm old enough to go to Chicago by myself.

159

There's a programme where they let kids fly by themselves – they call them UMs. Undercover Minors? No, Unidentified Minors. No—'

'Unaccompanied Minors!' Jonah screams out from his room.

'Thanks!' I yell back. 'Jonah told me that his friend Isaac takes airplanes by himself to visit his dad, and he's only seven. Can I do that to visit Nana?'

'Oh, honey! By yourself? Are you sure you're up for that?'

I nod. If I can navigate the deepest part of the ocean, I can definitely get around the airport. I don't say that part to my mum.

'You wouldn't find it scary?'

'I might,' I say. 'But being a little scared is worth it to see Nana.'

Mum sighs. 'I'll tell you what – I don't know much about this UM programme, but it sounds like a possibility. I'll look into it, okay?'

'Thanks, Mum. I can do it, I swear.'

'I have no doubt that you can,' she says softly. She inhales deeply. 'You smell delicious. Like the beach.'

I laugh. I can't help it.

She looks at me curiously. 'Do you have a suntan?'

'Er, no,' I say. 'It's just the light.'

She nods and tousles my hair. 'Maybe when all this work is finished, we should go to Florida for a week off.'

'Sounds good to me,' I say. She may wonder where we got our new swimming things.

'Hey, honey, why aren't you wearing any pyjamas?'

'Oh…um…' I think back to the story of *The Emperor's New Clothes*. If I tell my mum I'm actually wearing pjs will she pretend to believe me? Probably not. 'They're too tight,' I say, suddenly inspired. 'I need new ones. I'm a growing girl, you know.'

'Oh, I know,' she says, and smiles. 'I'll have to take you shopping. Now go and get dressed and then come down for breakfast, 'kay? Time for school.'

I nod. Even though I'm tired, I'm excited to see Frankie and Robin. I wish I could tell them what I've been up to, but I don't think we're supposed to tell anyone.

Hmm. Are we not supposed to tell anyone, or just not our parents?

Could I bring Frankie and Robin with us next time? Would the mirror let them in?

Once my mum leaves, I jump out of bed and pick up my jewellery box.

Lana is no longer a mermaid. Instead, she has legs. She's lying on her stomach, propped up by her elbows, wearing a yellow sundress and strappy sandals.

She's writing in a notebook.

She's a real writer! Yay!

I wonder if she found a worthy prince. Or maybe a worthy surfer. I wonder if I'll ever see her again. I wonder where the mirror will take me next.

I study the other characters on my jewellery box. I've always wanted to meet Sleeping Beauty. And Rapunzel. And that flying carpet really does look like fun. I'll just have to hold on extra tight.

I'm ready, Maryrose. For answers. For excitement. For our next adventure. Wherever it may be.

Acknowledgements

Thank you to my awesome agents, publishers, first readers, and friends: Laura Dail, Tamar Rydzinski, Brian Lipson, Aimee Friedman, Abby McAden, David Levithan, Becky Shapiro, Becky Amsel, Bess Braswell, Allison Singer, Janet Robbins, Elizabeth Parisi, Lizette Serrano, Emily Heddleson, Candace Greene, AnnMarie Anderson, Courtney Sheinmel, Emily Bender, Anne Heltzel, Lauren Myracle, E. Lockhart, Tori, Carly and Carol Adams, Avery and Whitney Carmichael, Targia Clarke, Jess Braun, Lauren Kisilevsky, Bonnie Altro, Susan Finkelberg-Sohmer, Corinne and Michael Bilerman, Debbie Korb, Joanna Steinberg, Casey Klurfeld, Jess Rothenberg, Adele Griffin, Leslie Margolis, Robin Wasserman, Maryrose Wood, Tara Altebrando, Sara Zarr, Ally Carter, Jennifer Barnes, Alan Gratz, Penny Fransblow, Maggie Marr, and Farrin Jacobs.

Love and thanks to my family: Aviva, Mom, Robert, Dad, Louisa, Gary, Lori, Sloane, Isaac, Vickie, John, Gary, Darren, Ryan, Jack, Jen, Teri, Briana, Michael,

David, Patsy, Murray, Maggie, and Jenny. Extra love and extra thanks and lots and lots of kisses to Chloe, Anabelle, and Todd.

Have you joined
Abby and Jonah for all
their journeys through
the magic mirror?

Read on for a taster of where
the adventure began in

FAIREST OF ALL

Mirror, Mirror, Bolted to the Wall

One step. *Creak.*

Two steps. *Creak!*

Three. *Creeeeeak!*

I stop on the very bottom stair and look across the basement at the huge and creepy mirror. It's still huge and creepy, but other than that, it looks perfectly fine. 'There is not a single crack in the mirror,' I say. 'We're going back to bed. Now.'

'I never said it was *cracked*,' Jonah says. 'I said it was hissing.' He approaches the mirror, getting so close his breath turns the glass foggy. 'It must have stopped when I left.'

I stay where I am, taking in every last detail of the antique mirror the previous owners left behind. It's twice the size of me. The glass part is clear and smooth. The frame is made of stone and decorated with carvings of small fairies with wings and wands. I don't know why the old owners didn't take it with them, except… well, it's creepy. And attached to the wall. With big, heavy Frankenstein bolts.

In the reflection I see my shoulder-length curly brown hair. My lime-green pyjamas. My striped slippers. Only, there's something off about my reflection, so I turn away. I don't know *what* exactly, but it's weird.

'It's not hissing,' I say, checking out the rest of the basement. Black leather sofa. Desk. Swivel chair. Lots and lots of bookshelves, all filled with my parents' old law books, which they never look at but don't want to throw away. Mum and Dad are both lawyers. Unlike me, neither of them wants to be a judge.

For the record: I'm going to be a really great judge because I'm all about peace and order. I'll make sure justice is always served, because it's not fair when bad people don't get in trouble, or when bad things happen to good people.

Like my parents making me move to Smithville.

'You have to knock,' Jonah says.

His words pull me back. 'What's that?'

'On the mirror,' he says, his eyebrows scrunching together. 'You have to knock.'

I laugh. 'I'm not knocking on the mirror! Why would anyone knock on a mirror?'

'They would if it was an accident! See, I was playing flying crocodile when—'

'What's flying crocodile?' I ask.

'An awesome new game I invented. I'm a pirate and I'm being chased by crocodiles, except my crocodiles can fly and—'

'Never mind,' I say, regretting I asked. 'How did this lead you to the mirror?'

'Well, when I was being chased by one of the flying crocodiles—'

'One of the *imaginary* flying crocodiles.'

'— when I was being chased by one of the *imaginary* flying crocodiles, I tripped and smacked into the not-imaginary mirror. It sounded like a knock. I'll do it again. Ready?'

Ready for what? I'm ready to get back into my toasty bed. But to him I say, 'Go ahead.'

He lifts his fist and knocks.

We wait. Nothing happens.

'Nothing's happening,' I tell him.

But then I hear a low hissing sound.

Sssssssssssssssssssssss.

My whole body tenses. I do not like hissing. Especially hissing mirrors. 'Um, Jonah?'

'See? Now check this out. Look what happens when I knock twice!'

He knocks again, and a warm light radiates from the mirror, too. A warm *purple* light.

'See?' Jonah says. 'Purple! Told you!'

My mouth goes dry. What is going on? Why is the mirror in our basement turning colours? Mirrors should not change colours. I do not like mirrors that change colours!

'This is when I went to get you. But I want to see what happens if I knock again. Three's a charm, right?'

'Jonah, no!'

Too late. He's already knocking.

Our reflection in the mirror starts to shake.

I don't like shaking mirrors any more than I like purple hissing mirrors.

'What's it doing?' I whisper. My image is rippling like the surface of a lake. My insides are rippling, too. Have I mentioned that I want to be a judge because I like peace? And order? And not rippling, hissing, purple-turning mirrors?!

'It's alive!' Jonah squeals.

The ripples in the mirror spin in a circle, like a whirlpool.

'We should go,' I say as tingles creep down my spine. 'Like, *now*.' I try to pull Jonah away, but I can't. Our images are churning around and around and around in the mirror like clothes in the dryer, and we're being dragged towards the mirror. Jonah's right foot slides forward. His trainer squeaks against the concrete floor.

'It wants my foot,' Jonah cries.

'Well, it can't have it!' I grab him tight. 'You can't have it, you…you mirror-thing!' I crane my neck toward the basement stairs. 'Mum! Dad!' I yell. But they are two floors up and I closed the basement door. Why did I close the basement door? I snuck into a basement in the middle of the night and closed the door? What is wrong with me? I need backup! 'Help!'

With my free hand I reach out and grasp the leg of the desk. My fingers burn, but I will absolutely not let go of my brother *or* the desk leg.

Whoosh! Suddenly, the whole world turns sideways. Jonah and I are horizontal. We wave in the air like human flags, which makes no sense. I don't like things that make no sense.

'Cool!' Jonah hollers. Is he smiling? He is! He's

smiling. How could he be having fun at a time like this?

My brother's shoe disappears. Disappears right off his foot and goes into the mirror.

No! Impossible!

There's a really loud buzzing, and my brother's other shoe gets swallowed by the mirror, too.

Slurp.

My heart is racing, and I'm hot and cold at the same time, because that could not have just happened. None of this can be happening. And why weren't Jonah's shoelaces tied? Do I have to do everything myself?

My slippers are suddenly sucked off my feet.

So not my fault. You can't tie slippers.

A book flies off the bookshelf and into the mirror. And another. All my parents' law books go – *swoop* – right off the bookshelf and into the mirror, their pages flapping like the wings of overexcited birds.

The swivel chair scoots across the floor. *Slurp!*

My brother's hands are slipping. 'Abby?' he says, and for the first time tonight, my brother – who isn't afraid of anything – sounds scared.

'Hold on!' I try to tighten my grip on his hand, but our palms are clammy. Pain shoots right from my fingers to my shoulders. I ignore it. I need to hold on. I *have* to hold on.

'Abby!'

'No!' I say, holding on even tighter. He flutters in the air. His eyes are wide and glowing purple.

'Jonah!' I scream. NO, NO, NO. I will NOT let the crazy mirror slurp up my brother. I'm in charge here! I will keep my brother safe!

I let go of the leg of the desk and grab him with both hands. With a satisfied grumble, the mirror sucks us both inside.

Read

to find out what happens next!